"Come on, Earl." Larco drifted beside him. "It's a ship right enough," he mused. "Maybe we should try getting in from the inside. The hold's open, if it is a hold, and maybe–" He broke off as the ground heaved beneath their feet. "A quake!"

It came again, and then a third time far more intense than before. Dumarest felt himself gripped by invisible forces and thrown high to one side, spinning, buffeted by shifting masses of water. The ship lifted, slowly, seemed to hesitate for a long moment and then fell back on the ledge. It slipped a little towards the edge of the chasm and then came to rest.

From the depths something rose like a plume of smoke.

It was an eel, attracted by the hammering, frightened by the sudden quake. The sinuous body was thirty feet long and spined like the edge of a saw. The barrel-sized head was crested, the gaping jaws lined with rows of gleaming teeth. It poised, watching the three men. Then like an arrow it sliced through the water, intent on its prey. . . .

The Dumarest of Terra Series
by E.C. Tubb, from Ace Science Fiction:

VERUCHIA

E. C. TUBB

SF
ACE BOOKS, NEW YORK

An Ace Book

Published by arrangement with the author

ISBN: 0-441-86181-4

First Ace Printing: June 1973
Second Printing: November 1982

Published simultaneously in Canada

Manufactured in the United States of America

Ace Books, 200 Madison Avenue, New York, New York 10016

For
Lisa Sharon Elcomb

I

There was something cathedral-like about the museum so that visitors walked softly and spoke in little more than whispers, awed by the nobility of the building. It was of natural stone, the high, vaulted roofs murmuring with distant echoes, the vast chambers flanked with galleries and long windows of brightly stained glass. Even the attendants standing unobtrusively beside carved pillars seemed more like exhibits than men: creatures subjected to the taxidermist's art, uniformed simulacra set to guard fabulous treasures. It would have been easy to have forgotten their presence.

Dumarest did not forget. From the moment he had entered the museum he had been conscious of their watchful eyes. They followed him now as he walked with a dozen others, his neutral gray in strong contrast to their city finery, a stranger and therefore an object of interest. Even guards grew bored.

"A phendrat." The voice of the guide rose above the sussuration of halting feet. He pointed upwards to where a winged and spined creature hung suspended on invisible wires. Even in death it radiated a vicious ferocity.

The treatment which had preserved it had not detracted from the glitter of its scales.

"The last of its species was destroyed over three centuries ago in the Tamar Hills. It was a carnivore and the largest insect ever known on this world: the result, apparently, of wild mutation. Its life cycle followed a standard pattern, the female sought out a suitable host and buried her eggs in the living flesh. See the sting? The venom paralyzed the selected creature which could do nothing as it was eaten alive by the hatching young. Note the long proboscis, the mandibles and the hooked legs. This is the sound of a phendrat in flight."

The guide touched a button set in a pillar and a thin, spiteful drone filled the air. A matron cleared her throat as it died away.

"Are you certain there are none left?"

"Positive, madam."

"I've a farm in the Tamar Hills. If I thought those things were still around I'd sell it tomorrow."

"You have nothing to fear, madam, I assure you." The guide moved on. "A krish," he said, halting beside a ten-foot display case filled with a mass of convoluted spines. "This one was found at the bottom of the Ashurian Sea. If you will study it you will see that the body-shell is almost covered with bright stones. Sometimes they are found so thickly laden that true mobility is lost. The stones are not natural to the creature and, as yet, we cannot determine whether or not the adornment is deliberate or accidental. By that I mean there is a possibility that the creature actually chooses to adorn its shell in the manner you see. If so the purpose could either be for camouflage, which seems unlikely, or as a means of attracting a mate."

"Like a girl dressing up?" The man was young and inclined to be frivolous.

The guide was curt. "Something like that, sir. But this is a male."

"But wouldn't that mean it is intelligent?" The girl had a thin, intent face with thick brows over eyes set a little too close for beauty. She glanced up at Dumarest and he noted, among other things, that she had stayed close to his side all through the tour. "Wouldn't you say that? I mean, if a creature exercises free choice doesn't that imply it has a thinking brain? And, if it can think, then it must be intelligent."

The guide moved on and saved him from the necessity of a reply. This time the man halted before a pedestal bearing a peculiar fabrication of metal.

"A mystery," he said. "The alloy is of a nature unused and contains traces of elements which are not native to this world. It was obviously part of a fabrication, a machine, possibly, but what the machine was or the part this played in its construction is unknown. It was found buried in alluvium and was discovered during the mining operations at Creen. Aside from the fact that it is very old and of an artificial nature nothing is known about it." He paused. "Of course there are rumors: an earlier native civilization which developed a high technology and then completely vanished without leaving any other trace; the discarded part of a spaceship of unknown manufacture; an art form of a culture unknown—the choice is limited only by the imagination. Personally I believe the explanation to be less bizarre."

The girl said, "And that is?"

"My own belief?" The guide shrugged. "The part of a machine which proved unsatisfactory and was reclaimed

11

for salvage. The alien elements could have been imported and the alloy was probably one of a series tested for greater efficiency. Economic pressure or the discovery of a cheaper substitute would account for it no longer being in use. It most likely fell from a raft during transport to a smelter."

A safe, mundane explanation, thought Dumarest, and one calculated to reduce interest in the strange fabrication. Who would be intrigued by junk? Yet he did not turn away, stepping closer to the pedestal instead and studying the near-shapeless mass with narrowed eyes. It was hopeless. The thing defied any attempt to determine its original function, the attrition of time marring its delicate construction. And it was delicate, that much was obvious despite the damage it had sustained: metal-like lace interspersed with solid elements and weaving conduits. If they were conduits. If the metal had originally been like lace.

"Old," said a voice quietly. The girl was still at his side. "So very old. Did you notice how the guide paid no attention to that in his explanation?"

"He probably didn't think it important."

"Do you?" Her voice held interrogation. "Are you interested in ancient things? Is that why you are visiting the museum?"

Dumarest wondered at her interest. Was it an attempt to make casual conversation or was it something deeper? She looked harmless enough, a young girl, a student perhaps, busy widening her education, but appearances could be deceptive.

"It was raining," he said. "The museum offered shelter. And you?"

"I've nothing better to do." Her voice fell a little,

gained a slight huskiness. "And you can meet such interesting people in a museum." Her hand slipped through his arm and held it close. Through her clothing he could feel the cage of her ribs, the feverish heat of her body. "Shall we catch up with the others or have you had enough?"

"And if I have?"

"There are more things to do on a rainy evening than look at the past." She paused and added, meaningfully, "More pleasant and just as educational. Well?"

"The guide is waiting," he said, and pulling his arm free strode down the chamber.

The man had halted before a cleared space ringed with a barrier of soft ropes curling from stanchions. One hand rested on a buttoned pedestal, the other was raised in a theatrical gesture.

"Your attention," he said as Dumarest, followed by the girl, joined the party. "What you are about to see is a true mystery for which even I have no explanation. First I will permit you to feast your eyes and then I will tell you what it is you see." He paused, a showman captivating his audience, then firmly pressed the button. "Behold!"

Later the balm of time and weather would soften the bleakness, rounding edges and blurring harsh contours, casting a net of vegetation over the place so that the ragged outlines would merge into the landscape and the ruins be transformed into an intriguing irregularity. But now the rawness was like a blow: a jumbled pile of desolation naked to the lavender sky, the tortuous striations of savage color stark against a somber background; the exposed entrails of a beast stricken with the blind fury of relentless destruction.

13

A city, thought Dumarest, like a machine, like a man, showed the agony of its death.

He stepped forward and felt the soft impact of the barrier against his thighs, blinking as he remembered that this was illusion, but the hologram was so lifelike that it deluded even as to scale. It was hard to remember that these were not real ruins a short distance away, that they need not even look exactly as they seemed.

Thickly he said, "Korotya?"

"The same." The guide sounded surprised. "An unusual sight as I think you will all agree, and one of the mysteries of Selend. No one knows how destruction came to this place. Even the existence of the city was unsuspected though there had been rumors. The site is unfit for husbandry and so attracted no settlers. Hunters must have stumbled on it from time to time but, if so, they never reported having found it. The assumption is that the inhabitants made sure they could not."

A woman said, sharply, "Killed them, you mean?"

"Possibly, but there is no proof."

To one side a girl whispered, "It's horrible. Such destruction! And yet, in a way, it's also magnificent. Those colors, those shapes, but how. . . ?"

"Atomics." Her companion was emphatic. "What else could have generated such heat? See how the stone has fretted into outflung traceries? Internal pressures must have done that, the superheated air on the interior gusting out to blast the molten walls. The varied colors must be due to internal structures, pipes, wires, reinforcements of diverse nature. The whole thing must have happened almost instantaneously. A tremendous blast of heat which reduced the entire area into what we see."

"But an entire city!" The girl echoed her disbelief. "And no one knew it was there?"

"No one," said the guide, then amended his flat statement. "Aside from the inhabitants, of course, assuming that there were any inhabitants. All we know is that fifty-eight years ago seismological instruments registered a shock of great proportions. Almost at the same time reports were received of a column of flame, oddly brief, which came from the point of disturbance. The two were obviously connected. Later investigation discovered what you see before you. The area was intensely radioactive and still precludes personal investigation. It will be another century before we dare move in to commence excavations but there is little doubt as to what we shall find."

Nothing. Circling the barrier Dumarest had no hope of anything else. The entire place must be fused solid—the buildings and the ground for miles around. There was no hope that records would remain, not even a carving on stone, a metal block engraved with the data he had hoped to find, certainly not a man who could tell him what he wanted to know.

A man's voice rose, puzzled. "I still can't understand how the place could have remained undiscovered. Surely there were flights over the area?"

"The entire area was mapped by aerial photography three times during the past two centuries."

"And nothing was seen?"

"Nothing." The guide was emphatic. "The terrain showed only an unbroken expanse of forest. As I said Korotya is a mystery. If there were answers to the questions which fill your minds it would be a mystery no longer. Those ruins are fifty-eight years old and that is

15

the only thing we can be sure about, the only real fact we have. All the rest is surmise. How long the city existed, who built it, who lived in it, how it was destroyed, these are things we do not know."

Dumarest had circled the area. As he approached the rest of the party the image flickered and abruptly vanished. Reaching forward he pressed the button on the pedestal and restored the illusion.

To the guide he said, "Some things can surely be determined. The destruction was atomic in nature—you mentioned residual radioactivity."

"That is so."

"I assume this world is monitored. Was any record made at the time of atmospheric flights or spatial approaches?"

The guide frowned. "I fail to understand you, sir."

"Could the area have been bombed?"

"Selend was not at war. The destruction was an isolated act and, in any case, how could anyone attack a city unless they knew exactly where it was? And what reason could there be for such willful destruction?"

Dumarest pressed the point. "You haven't answered my question. Would you agree that the city could have been destroyed by external forces?"

"It could have been," admitted the guide reluctantly. "But, equally so, it could have been destroyed in other ways. An internal explosion, for example. An experiment which went wrong—there are a multitude of possible explanations, but all of them must remain pure surmise. As I said, Korotya is a mystery." He looked at Dumarest. "You have other questions?"

Dumarest made his decision. He had come too far not

tó ask even though he could guess the answer. But he had nothing to lose.

"One," he said. "You mentioned that there were many rumors—did one of them have anything to do with the Original People?"

"Sir?"

"A religious sect maintaining a strict seclusion. Could Korotya have been their home?"

Blandly the guide said, "Anything is possible, sir, but I have never heard of the sect you mention." He raised his voice. "And now, ladies and gentlemen, if you will please follow me into the other chamber I will show you the original coronation garments of the first ruler of Selend. We no longer have a monarchy, of course but Ellman Conde was a very unusual man and insisted on wearing a very unusual robe."

His voice faded to a murmur as he led the way, the others of the party following, the girl with the thin face hesitating and then, shrugging, following the rest. Alone Dumarest stared at the enigmatic ruins.

He had arrived sixty years too late.

A rumor picked up on a distant world had brought him to Selend and it had been a wasted journey. Once again as the image died he restored the illusion, looking intently at the harsh destruction. It had been too big for a monastery and there was too much stone for it to have been a simple village tucked beneath sheltering trees. Those trees and the topsoil would have been burned away, vaporized, exposing what lay beneath. Much of what he saw would have lain underground but it was still too large for primitive commune. Art, skill and technology had gone into its construction and now it was dead and those who had lived and worked in it must be dead also. And with them the knowledge he had hoped to obtain.

He turned from the display as a fresh party led by a vociferous guide came towards him. It had stopped raining and he hesitated at the doors of the museum, looking at the gleaming streets, slickly wet beneath the lights. It was still early, people crowding the sidewalk, traffic thick on the pavements: a normal city on a normal, highly developed world. A place in which he felt restless and had no real part. His skin crawled to the imagined touch of invisible chains.

Casually he looked around. A cluster of young girls, their voices like the twitter of birds as they chatted, waiting for friends. A tall, slim young man with a tuft of beard wearing orange and purple. A fat man arguing with his wife. An oldster, stooped, coughing and spitting phlegm. Two thick-set types, artisans probably, standing side by side silent and watchful.

A Hausi came running up the stairs, his face marked with tribal scars. He hesitated as he saw Dumarest as if about to speak, his eyes curious, then he passed on into the museum. Dumarest turned, watching him through the glass as he moved quickly towards the offices, wondering what such a man was doing on so remote a world. Hausia rarely strayed far from the center of the galaxy where worlds were thick and their skills appreciated.

He moved as a crowd of adolescents thronged towards the doors, running lightly down the stairs and across the street. He kept to the busy ways heading towards the edge of the city and his hotel. A tout called softly as he neared a lighted doorway.

"Lonely, mister? There's plenty of fun inside. Genuine

feelies of a thousand kinds. Full sensory participation and satisfaction guarenteed. Why live it when you can feel it? All the thrills and none of the dangers. No?" He shrugged philosophically as Dumarest passed, raising his voice again a moment later, falling silent almost immediately.

Dumarest frowned. A tout would not break his spiel without reason; win or lose he would try every prospect, picking them out with the skill of long training, the lonely, the strangers away from home, those who looked as if they could be lured into his parlor. Someone must be close behind, a person intent on business, not pleasure.

Deliberately he slowed, ears strained, listening for the scuff of feet. There was too much noise and he heard nothing definite. He slowed even more; if the man were genuine he would maintain his pace and pass. He did neither.

Dumarest halted, tense, belated caution pricking its warning.

He felt the sting of something against the back of his head, the impact, and spun, left arm outstretched, the fingers extended and clamped so as to form a rigid whole. Light from an overhead standard turned the stone of his ring into a streak of ruby fire. He saw the man standing behind him, the face pale and startled over the tuft of beard, then his fingers hit, catching the eye, ripping and tearing at yielding flesh. The man shrieked and fell away as, carried by his own momentum, Dumarest continued to turn, his neck already stiff, his legs unresponsive.

The screams of the injured man followed him as he fell to the concrete an infinite distance below.

He awoke to a glare of light.

"All right, nurse," said a heavy voice. "The primary was successful." The light moved aside and was replaced by a broad, dark face topped with a green cap bearing a medical insignia. "You've nothing to worry about," soothed the doctor. "The danger is past and you're going to be perfectly well. Now I want you to cooperate. Please blink your eyes, left first then right. That's it. Again, please. Once more. Good. Now follow the movements of my finger." He made satisfied noises as Dumarest obeyed. "Now move your head. Excellent. You may give him the secondary now, nurse."

Dumarest felt something touch the side of his neck and he heard the sharp hiss as air blasted drugs into his bloodstream. The reaction was immediate. Life and feeling returned to his limbs, his lungs heaved beneath his aching ribs. He sat upright, fighting a sudden wave of nausea, resting his head in his hands until it had passed.

"To ask how you feel would be a stupid question," said the doctor conversationally. "You have been under artificial stimulation for almost two weeks and the machines are not always gentle. But you are alive and the discomfort will pass."

"Thank you," said Dumarest. "For saving my life."

"You were fortunate in more ways than one. The screams of the man you injured attracted the police. They immediately summoned an ambulance. The medical orderly gave you quick-time to slow your metabolism and put you in freeze." The doctor paused as if wondering whether to say more. "I found a dart buried in your scalp. It bore traces of a substance which took our medical computer some time to isolate and more to determine a neutralizing compound. The difficulty was in maintaining life while it took effect; hence the use of the machines."

"I understand," said Dumarest. "And the man?"

"The one you injured?" The doctor shrugged. "Dead. Not from his injury, you merely tore his eye, but from other causes."

"Such as?"

"Cardiac failure." The doctor became brusque. "We have talked long enough. Now you had better rest for a while in order to recover your strength. But do not be concerned. You have nothing to worry about."

Nothing, thought Dumarest as the man left followed by the nurse. Nothing aside from the fact that someone had tried to kill him and would probably try again.

Rising from the bed he crossed to where curtains hid a window. It was no surprise to find it barred. He stood looking out at the night, the reflection of his face limned against the clouded sky. It had been raining again and tiny droplets made miniature rainbows against the panes. He touched the back of his head. The wound had healed; aside from that he had no proof that time had passed at all.

He lowered his eyes. The room was set high in the building and the view stretched across an ugly cluster of roads, stores and huddled buildings to where the spacefield glowed beneath its circle of lights. As he watched a ship lifted upwards, bright in the glowing field of its Erhaft drive as it reached towards the stars. Again he looked at the city. Limitless space and worlds without number spread across the galaxy. Why did men insist on building their habitations so close?

Turning from the window he studied the room. A bed, an empty cabinet, toilet facilities and nothing else. He wore nothing but a loose hospital robe, his only personal possession the ring on his left hand. At least they had left him that. The door was unlocked. He opened it and met the flat stare of an armed guard seated in the passage outside. Slowly the man shook his head.

Closing the door Dumarest returned to the bed and eased the aching muscles of his body. He was a prisoner. There was nothing to do now but wait.

They kept him waiting for two days and then returned his clothes and took him to the place of interrogation. It could be no other than that, a room in which someone would ask questions and demand answers and, if there were no instruments of persuasion to be seen, it was no proof that they did not exist or would not be used. Most probably they had been used; a drugged man could retain few secrets.

"Dumarest." The man sitting at the wide desk was of indeterminate age, his face smooth, bland, his body almost as slight as that of a boy. He picked up a card lying before him. "Earl Dumarest, traveler, arrived on Selend seventeen days ago from . . . ?" He paused, looking up. His eyes were gray flecked with motes of blue.

"Onsul."

"And before that?"

"Vington."

"Which you reached from Technos." The examiner smiled, his teeth very white and very pointed. "I am glad that you are being sensible, Earl. I may call you that? My name is Cluj. Please be seated." He waited as Dumarest took a chair. "What is your planet of origin?"

"Earth."

"A strange name for a world. There is no record of it in our files, but no matter, there are so many worlds." Without change of tone or expression he said, "Why did you come to Selend?"

"To visit Korotya." If he had been questioned under drugs there was no point in lying and it was obvious now that he had. Else why should Cluj have checked on Earth? "I had heard of the place, a rumor, and I wanted to see it."

"Why?"

"I was curious."

"About the Original People?" The examiner leaned back in his chair, smiling. "I know all that you have done since your arrival. The guide at the museum remembers you well. A great pity that you traveled so far to learn so little. You saw the ruins."

"I saw a hologram of ruins," corrected Dumarest.

"You are precise and wise to be so, but I assure you the depiction was genuine. Korotya, unfortunately, is lost to us forever." Cluj picked up the card and began to rap the edge softly on his desk. "The Original People," he mused. "A minor religious sect holding strange beliefs and conducting esoteric ceremonies. They claim that we all originated on one planet." He looked at Dumarest. "Earth. Are you one of them?"

"No."

"And yet you seek to find them, is that it? If you thought they were here you were mistaken. We do not tolerate such misguided fanatics on Selend. And the city, the ruins of Korotya, can you honestly believe that such people could have built it and kept it hidden for so long? The thing is against reason."

Cluj threw down the card. "Now let us deal with a more important matter. The attack on your person is something which disturbs me. It is a puzzle and I do not like puzzles. It was not a simple attempt at robbery and neither was it a thwarted assassination. Later analysis has shown that the poison fed into your blood was not intended to kill but to paralyze. A most sophisticated compound and one beyond the reach of any ordinary criminal. Its effect is to render a person immediately helpless with all the apparent symptoms of death. Now why should you be attacked in such a manner?"

"A case of mistaken identity, perhaps?"

"It is barely possible," conceded the examiner. "Such things happen. Unfortunately we cannot question the man who fired the dart into your scalp. He is dead."

"So I heard," said Dumarest dryly. "The doctor told me the cause was cardiac failure."

"He did not lie."

"Maybe not, but there are many ways to stop a heart from beating."

"True, in this case it was a hole burned with a laser." Cluj leaned forward across his desk. "You realize what this means? The man was not working alone. It was a planned attempt and if you hadn't been so cautious it would have succeeded. You would simply have vanished without trace. A stranger, collapsing in the street—who would have questioned either the incident or the disposal of the body? And if they tried once they could well try again." He paused as if waiting for Dumarest to comment and, when he remained silent, added, "I will be frank with you. The episode carries political implications, a potential danger we can do without. Selend must not become a battleground for warring factions."

Dumarest said, quietly, "You overexaggerate the matter. I still think that I was mistaken for someone else."

"If you think that then you are a fool and I do not take you for a fool. I believe that you realize perfectly the implications of what has occurred. You have enemies and you are not the type of man to suffer injury unavenged. However, that is not my concern or will cease to be very soon. I will be blunt. You are no longer welcome on this world. I have ordered your deportation."

Dumarest relaxed. "There is no need for you to take official action. I will leave as soon as I find a suitable ship."

"The matter has been arranged."

"Not to my satisfaction," snapped Dumarest. "I am not a criminal and this is a civilized world. I demand the right to book my own passage."

"And how will you pay for it?" Cluj watched as Dumarest pulled back his left sleeve and revealed the tattoo on his arm. The metallic imprint of his universal credit shone in the light. Quietly he said, "I would not leave any man totally destitute. You have, perhaps, enough left to maintain you for a week in a modest hotel."

Dumarest lowered his sleeve. His face was hard, taut with anger. "I had cash, also. Does Selend put uniforms on its thieves?"

Cluj was offended. "You were not robbed. There was a matter of paying certain expenses: the cost of your hospitalization, the research needed to neutralize the poison, other things. The price of a long High passage for one. The cash and credit barely sufficed. You will, naturally, receive a full accounting." He spoke into a grille on his desk. "This interview is terminated. Collect the subject and deal with him as arranged." To Dumarest he said, "You leave at dawn. Do not return to Selend."

They took him to the spacefield, to a small building set within the barrier, a place used for holding undesirable transients. The cell was small, clean enough but cramping to a man used to open spaces. From the single barred window Dumarest could see the field, the ships tall against the darkening sky. One of them would carry him from Selend and dump him where? The guard either did not know or had orders to remain silent.

"Don't worry about it, friend," he advised. "You'll travel just like an ordinary passenger. Quick-time to shorten the journey and all the rest of it. What does it matter where the ship is bound?"

It mattered. Too many worlds were at the end of the line, dead ends without industry or offering any hope of being able to build a stake. Such worlds were a traveler's nightmare. Stranded, without money to buy a passage, it was almost impossible to escape. Death in abject poverty was the usual end. Had Cluj chosen to send him to one of those? Or was he being even more direct?

Dumarest thought about it while sitting on the narrow bunk. His deportation had been planned, his money taken while he lay unconscious in the hospital. Had someone suggested that course of action? Advised it? Used pressure to win what they had tried to gain by the attack? Was he to be delivered, an unsuspecting parcel, into the hands of the hunters?

It was a risk he dared not take. Somehow he had to break free of the suspected trap. From the window he studied the vessels spaced on the field. Five of them; Selend was a busy world. One stood with gaping plates, obviously undergoing overhaul or repair. He eliminated it. Another had just arrived, the loading ports open, cargo streaming down the ramp to waiting vehicles. It was barely possible that it could off-load, restock and leave at dawn but he doubted it. One of the remaining three must be the ship on which he was booked, but which?

Carefully he studied them. One was sealed, the cargo loaded and the ship apparently ready to leave. Captains did not favor delay—once ready for space they seldom lingered—yet the crew could be enjoying a short leave now that the work was done. The other two were still loading, one with a stream of heavy bales, the other with a trickle of smaller bundles. Some men clustered at the foot of the ramp, poorly dressed, huddled as if for mutual protection. Travelers hoping for a Low passage.

Thoughtful, Dumarest turned from the window and stared at the barred door of his cell. It was a minor barrier compared to another. How to escape without money? Who on those ships would give him passage as a gift? He knew the answer too well. Then he looked at his ring, the thick band and the flat stone which shone like freshly spilled blood. Cluj had made a mistake.

He waited until dark and then hammered at the barred door. The guard came, grumbling, wiping his mouth with the back of his hand. He was a big man, thickly muscled and inclined to be truculent. His manner softened a little as he heard what Dumarest had to say.

"You want some wine and a good meal? Well, I guess it could be arranged if you've the money to pay for it."

"I've got credit." Dumarest displayed his tattoo. "If you've got a banking machine we could cash it and get something decent to eat and drink. Look," he urged as the man hesitated. "What can you lose? I'll transfer the credit to your account and you give me two-thirds in value."

"Two-thirds?"

"Make it a half. Just bring the machine here and we'll do it right away. I'm starving."

The guard rubbed thoughtfully at his chin. "I can't do that, bring the machine here, I mean. It's a fixture in the office. I guess I could take you down to it, though. A half, you say?"

It was a good profit and he would make more by bolstering the price of the food and wine. And it was safe enough, a short journey to the office and then back to the cell. Five minutes, ten at the most; the opportunity was too good to be missed.

"All right," he decided. "But don't try anything smart. We don't want to put you aboard with a busted head." Unlocking the door of the cell he gestured down the passage. "Turn right at the end," he ordered. "And let's make this fast."

Dumarest hit him on the jaw.

It was a hard blow, delivered with the full force of back and shoulders, and the man slumped as if he'd been shot. Dumarest caught the sagging body, pushed it into the cell and slammed the door. Quietly he entered the office. It was empty and he took time to glance at the papers littering the desk. The *Lachae* was due to leave at dawn.

The rain had started again, sleeting drops making a curtain of silver beneath the glare of the circling lights. They stung his eyes as Dumarest left the office and raced across the field. Ahead lay the two ships he had spotted earlier, loading finished now, one with a savage red light winking from its prow. He reached it, climbed the ramp and met the hostile stare of the handler.

"What the hell do you want?" The man was abrupt. "We're just getting ready to leave."

"Good. I want passage."

"The old man takes care of that."

"Low, not High." Dumarest looked around. He was in the lower section close to the cargo and freeze. A bench stood to one side, a vice clamped to the surface. Slipping off his ring he tore the stone free with his teeth and put it between the jaws. He threw the band towards the handler and, as the man examined it, tightened the jaws of the vice.

The stone shattered into a million crystalline shards.

"Are you crazy?" The handler stared at the glittering fragments. "Ruining a stone like that!"

Dumarest was curt. "Forget the stone. Look at the band. It's worth a High-passage. It's yours if you'll carry me Low."

The handler was well past youth, shrewd with much experience of men. He looked calculatingly at Dumarest as he weighed the ring in his hand. "You're running from trouble, eh? Well, it's none of my business. We're bound for Dradea. It's a hell of a long journey but that won't bother you the way you'll be traveling." He bounced the weight of metal in his hand. "Just a warning, friend. If this is a phony you'll pay for it."

With callous indifference, denied the numbing drugs which would ease the pain of resurrection so that he would scream his lungs raw with the pain of returning circulation. That and other things. Those riding Low had no defense against a handler full of spite or turning sour.

"It's genuine," said Dumarest.

"And all you have?" The handler shrugged. "Well, that's the way it goes. You've ridden Low before? Good. Then you know what to do."

To strip and lie in a cabinet designed for the transportation of animals. To sink into oblivion and ride doped, frozen and ninety percent dead, gambling his life against the fifteen percent death rate. He had done it so often before. Too often. Maybe this time would be the last.

A man's luck could not last forever.

II

Veruchia came late to the stadium, leaving it until the last possible moment when to delay further would be beyond excuse and taken as a deliberate insult. That would be both stupid and unwise; policy dictated that she should have been at her place in the high box long ago and yet, at times, personal feelings made it hard to be so calculating. So she compromised. She would be there and would make certain that she was seen, but not even for the rule of a world would she subject herself to greater degradation.

Trumpets sounded as she passed the guards, her footsteps loud in the following hush as she climbed the stairs. She slowed a little, reluctant to witness what was taking place, conscious even here beneath the stands of the anticipation above. But there was no escape. As she climbed the final steps and stood blinking in the brilliant sunlight she heard the roar of the crowd. It was deafening, the sound of thirty thousand people yelling as one, and their voice was the hungry scream of a beast: an animal gloating at the sight of blood and demanding more.

It was contagious, that demand. She felt raw, primitive

emotions stir her blood despite her contempt for the games and shook herself, angrily, making for her chair. Even so her eyes betrayed her, glancing at the arena where men ran forward with nets and tridents, seeing the broken shape and the carmine pool. Quickly she looked at the other occupants of the box, seeing what she had expected, a vague hope that others would have had the strength to register their disapproval fading as she counted heads.

Chorzel was there, naturally, his great body crammed into the royal seat, his face that of a graven image, unmoving, his eyes mere slits in the puffed contours of his face. She glanced at his hands, frowning as she saw the thick fingers clamped to the arms of his chair, the skin taut over the knuckles. Quickly she glanced back at his face. It was beaded with sweat, a tiny rivulet of perspiration running from his forehead down over one cheek to stain the gaudy fabric circling his throat. Her frown deepened. It was hot, true, but Chorzel did not usually suffer from the heat and he was most certainly not a man to bear discomfort without need. Was he so enamored of what lay on the sand that he could not lift a hand to wipe his face?

It was possible and again she wondered what had made him turn the relatively harmless games into the present disgusting spectacle. The given reasons she knew —she had heard them all too often and in too minute detail—but still she refused to be convinced. Yet how could she be so certain that she was right and he and the others wrong? The populace, at least, seemed to bear out his theories and so did their rulers. Vidda, for example; the woman looked as if she had just left the arms of a lover, her cheeks flushed, her eyes glazed, her body redolent of sensual passion.

And Selkas? He looked as he always did, utterly detached, casual, bland in his armor of cynical amusement. The smooth skin of his cheeks belied his age and yet he must be as old as Chorzel. Not for the first time she wondered what had made him drop all aspirations to power and adopt the habits of a dilettante.

She tried to catch his attention, failed, and turned as a hand fell on her knee. The contact was distasteful and she squirmed as she knocked it aside. Montarg, smiling without humor, lifted his voice above the noise.

"You look disturbed, my cousin. Is your stomach so weak that you cannot stand the sight of a little blood?"

Coldly she said, "I do not regard the death of men as amusing."

"But educational, surely? See how the people enjoy it. Listen to them shout. Does not that teach you something about human nature, my dear?" He laughed, soundlessly like a dog, mouth wide to show the redness of his throat, the gleaming whiteness of his teeth. "If you were more of a woman, Veruchia, you would not be so unmoved. Look at Vidda, at Loris, even Nita finds within herself the capability to respond. But you look as if made of ice. Water must flow in your veins. No wonder that when men talk of you they smile."

"At least they do not spit."

"Can you be sure of that, cousin?"

He was baiting her as he always did, as he had done when, as children, they had played in the gardens of the palace. Then she had learned the mistake of displaying anger. He reveled in the fury of the helpless.

Quietly she said, "You are a sadist, Montarg. But from me you will get little pleasure."

"A sadist, cousin?"

"A sadist," she repeated. "And worse, a coward. You watch others die and gain pleasure from their pain. If you are genuinely entranced by the mystique of combat why aren't you in the arena strengthening your skill? Could it be that you are reluctant to put your manhood to the test?"

He refused to be annoyed. "Unlike yours, my dear, my sex is beyond question. And still you insist on missing the point of the games, as you so willfully insist on missing much that concerns the welfare of Dradea. You have a limited mind, cousin, but that is to be expected. A limited mind in a limited body. A lover, perhaps, could teach you something. You should try one." He paused then added, with deliberate cruelty, "I'm sure you could find someone to share your bed if you really tried. A cripple, perhaps, or a man unable to see."

He had beaten her as he always did. Eyes smarting, she turned from his smiling face as the crowd roared. An attendant nursed an arm streaming with blood. Belev, Montarg's satellite, grunted his impatience.

"The fool should have taken better care. And all of them are taking too long."

Montarg said, lazily, "Then urge them on."

Belev grinned and moved away. The sharp blast of a trumpet followed his order, imperious, demanding. Down in the arena they heard it and worked harder than before, ringing the crell with nets and tridents, taking wild risks as they forced it back so that others could lift the body of the dead man and carry it away. Lithe boys flung themselves at the stained sand, raking it smooth, burying the soiling blood beneath the golden grains.

In the comparative coolness and gloom of the preparation chamber the note sounded clear and threatening. A medical attendant grunted and said, "They're getting impatient out there. Trust Montarg for that. He believes in getting full value for his money. It's a wonder he didn't have us build a conveyor belt."

Sadoua scowled; at such times graveyard humor was out of place. Quickly he glanced at the waiting contestants; some had responded with a shrug and a strained smile, a few laughed with forced bravado.

Dumarest did neither.

He sat on a bench, relaxed, eyes half-closed and breathing with a deep, controlled rhythm. The bones of his ribs stood clear against his chest, his muscles limned beneath the hard whiteness of his skin. To many he looked as if half-asleep but the fightmaster knew better. This was a man preparing himself for battle, a coiled spring ready to explode into action: a man who had chosen to fight for money accepting the penalty of maiming or death if he failed.

Sadoua limped towards him. "You're next."

"Now?"

"Soon." The fightmaster was a squat man, a scar running over one cheek, more in parallel lines across his naked torso. He was sweating, thick droplets clinging to the hairs of his forked beard. He stepped aside as the men carrying the stretcher trotted past and swore as he looked at the mess it contained. "The fool. I told him to watch the feet. A crell kicks forward, not back. Watch beak and feet, I told him. You all heard me. Why didn't the damned fool listen?"

Dumarest rose, stretching. "Maybe he forgot."

"Forgot!" The fightmaster spat. "You only forget once in the arena. He should have known that. He told me that he'd fought before and promised a good show. A child could have done as well." He cocked his head at a roar from the crowd. "Listen to that. They're getting ugly. They paid to see good fighting, sharp, clear action, not a bunch of suicides. Do you think I like to see men walk out and dead meat carried in? Five so far, three more dying and four who'll never be the same again. And not a crell to show for it."

"You'd like to see one hit the sand?"

"More than one." Sadoua scowled and spat. "I've no love for those damn things. Don't get me wrong, the arena's my life, but in the old days it was different. Men against men, clubs, armor, that sort of thing. A man could get hurt, sure, but no one ever left his guts spread over the sand. Then things changed. Animals came in, bulls at first and then the big cats." Reflectively he rubbed the scars on his chest. "And then they brought in those damned birds. Even so a man stood a fair chance at first. Then they began to breed for size, weight and viciousness and now—" He broke off, conscious that he was saying too much. The morale of a fighter was important to his survival.

Gruffly he said, "A crell is just an overgrown bird. You can take it."

"If I don't it will take me."

"A good thing to remember." Sadoua glanced down the passage towards the arena. "Like a shot of something before you go? Some figure that it helps."

Dumarest shook his head.

"You're wise. I never touched it myself before a bout. After, yes, but never before. No matter what they say it can slow you down a little and that could be fatal." He led the way to where a door opened on the sand, halting at the edge of sunlight. "Don't forget now, watch those feet. A crell moves fast so try and get some sand into its eyes and slow it down. Don't stand facing it too long. Keep moving and—" He broke off as the tumpets blared. "Good luck!"

It was impossible to look away.

Veruchia sat on the edge of her seat, despising herself and yet trapped by the moment. The deadly fascination of the games, she thought. The anticipation, the accelerated pounding of the heart, the tension of nerve and sinew as if she herself were down there on the sand. The vicarious pleasure which filled the stands. The druglike euphoria which caused men and women to act like beasts. Yet how could she really blame them? They merely took what was provided, the danger faced by a surrogate, obvious, visible, while they sat safe and secure high above. As she was sitting now.

She felt the pressure in her lungs as the trumpets died, the sigh rising from thirty thousand throats, the rustle as bodies moved forward, heads craning towards the sand. And all of it was physical, a thing felt deep in bone and muscle, the allure of the arena, the beast of which she was a part.

Beside her Selkas drew in his breath.

"I know that man," he whispered incredulously. "I've seen him before, years ago now, but I could never forget."

She felt the touch of his cheek, as light as a feather, the urgent whisper of his voice in her ear.

"Veruchia, trust me. This is a golden chance for revenge against Montarg. Take it. Bet all you own on the fighter. It will be a wager you cannot lose."

Whispering she said, "Why are you so generous?"

"Why don't I make the bet myself?" His voice echoed his amusement. "A shrewd comment, but I have all the money I need. You need more than money. The taste of revenge is, I assure you, wonderfully sweet. Back the man against the crell and do it quickly before they engage. I doubt if this bout will take long."

She hesitated, watching the lone figure walking slowly across the sand. Her eyes were good and details were plain: his height, the scarred torso, the hard determination of his face—the face of a man who had long since learned to live outside of the protection of House or Guild, Family or Organization. A loner as, in a sense, was she. Looking at the man she felt a quick affinity. He like herself, faced tremendous odds. Perhaps if she backed him it might, in some unguessable way, help him, give him strength. And she had never had cause to doubt Selkas's good regard

"Quickly, Veruchia," he whispered. "Quickly."

Montarg's voice made her decision. "A thousand on the crell. A kill within three minutes."

Belev laughed. "Make it one and you're on."

"Three," Montarg insisted. "At his rate of progress he'll take all day to get within range." His voice grew hard. "I'll have a word with Sadoua about this. His choice of cattle is too poor to be tolerated."

Cattle! To talk so about men!

Veruchia turned and to Montarg said, "A wager, cousin?"

"You Veruchia? You want to make a bet?" His surprise was genuine then, recovering, he gave his soundless laugh. "Could it be that the heat of the sun is making you human? Do you thrill to the anticipation of blood?"

"You have a large mouth, cousin," she said coldly. "And words are cheap. Will you accept my wager?"

"On the crell?"

"The man. You will give me odds?"

He pondered, looking down at the arena, seeing only a trained and vicious crell and a man walking towards his destruction. The bird was from his own hatchery; he knew the strain and had no doubt as to the outcome. Veruchia must be insane—perhaps the atmosphere had turned her brain. In any case it was not a chance to be missed.

"You have an estate to the north adjoining my own. Against it I will set three times its market value."

"Only three?" Her shrug was expressive.

"Five then."

"You are cautious, Montarg." Already she was beginning to regret her wildness. Aside from a house in town the estate was all she had, apart from some land to the south, barren and of little value. Perhaps, if she pushed the odds high enough, she would force him to refuse the wager. How high? Eight? Ten? "Give me twelve and I will agree."

"Done." He spoke quickly; the man was getting close to the bird, delay might mean a lost opportunity. And what did the odds matter when the result was a foregone conclusion? "You are a witness, Selkas. And you, Vidda."

"Be silent," snapped the woman. She was breathing

41

raggedly, her hands clenched. "I am watching the conflict."

She and all the rest.

Dumarest could feel their eyes, sense the hunger, the savage desire for blood and action, the straining anticipation he had known so often before. A small ring with men facing each other with naked blades or a luxurious arena with men facing beasts, it was all the same. Aside from scale the audience never differed. All had the same hunger; all made the same demand.

He ignored them as he walked slowly across the sand, eyes on the crell. He was naked aside from a loincloth, the sun hot on his back and shoulders, burning beneath the soles of his feet. He carried an eight-foot spear as his only weapon and he knew that the length had been carefully judged. He could throw it—once. If he missed or if the blow did not kill he would never get a second chance. He could use it to thrust but that meant shortening the length to allow for holding, and if he used it as a quarterstaff he would have to get within the range of beak and feet.

He slowed a little, halting as the crell moved. It stood five feet high, the long neck lifting the head another three, a rounded ball of muscle coated with tough feathers, the claws like steel, the beak a living spear. It moved again, hopping to one side, the dry rasp of the furrowed sand oddly loud in the hushed silence. It froze, watching, its eyes close-set, reptilian, hypnotic in their stare.

It charged.

It came without warning, one second immobile, the next blasting forward as if shot from a gun, sand pluming from beneath its feet, neck outstretched, feathers bristling on vestigal wings. Dumarest sprang to one side, landing catlike, poised on the balls of his feet, the spear lifted in both hands. There was no time to use the weapon. Barely had he landed than the crell charged again, turning, ripping the sand, one clawed foot slashing at the space in which he had stood.

Dumarest ran for his life.

He heard the roar of the crowd as he raced down the arena, savage, angry at being robbed of their spectacle. He saw the gaping mouth of the door leading to the preparation chamber, Sadoua's scarred visage, the men standing on platforms to either side, spears poised to bring him down should he come too close. He leaped to one side, jumping high, turning in the air so that he faced back the way he had come, the spear gripped in both hands, leveling as he landed.

The crell had not followed. It strutted at the far end beneath the high box, head high, arrogant as it tore at the sand. From the crowd came a storm of jeers at what they regarded as cowardice.

A girl, young and pretty, her face disfigured with ugly passion, screamed, "Give him the whip! Lash the dog until he bleeds!"

Others took up the cry. Sadoua shook his head as an attendant touched his arm. "No. Not yet. That man is fighting for his life."

"But the crowd?"

"To hell with them! They want blood, not skill. Can't they realize that he was testing the crell to see what it could do? Now shut up and watch!"

Dumarest thrust the spear into the sand, dropped to one knee and rubbed his hands in the grit, his eyes never leaving the crell. Still it strutted back and forth, beak weaving, shining in the sun. Snakelike it poised as Dumarest rose and hefting the spear began to move slowly towards it.

Hushed, the crowd waited.

It was a thing, a beast bred for a certain task, natural attributes accentuated for a desired end. But it was still a beast with a limited brain governed more by instinct than calculated decision. Dumarest concentrated on it as he crossed the sand. There would be a point beyond which he could not pass without being attacked. An invisible line which was the creature's territorial limit. Anything crossing it would be attacked, viciously, without delay or warning. But, unless maddened by the scent of blood, the bird would probably not attack at a greater distance.

He remembered the girl, her screamed demands that he be whipped until he bled. A man could not hope to escape by staying a safe distance.

If there were a safe distance. If the crell would be content to stay in one place.

Looking at the increasing movement of the feet Dumarest knew that it would not. It would strut the length of the arena, its present domain, and inevitably he would get too close.

Still he advanced.

He had the spear, his hands and feet, his brain. He could think and calculate, the age-old advantage a man had over a beast. He could anticipate and prepare and act when the moment came. His life depended on his judgment.

The crell twitched then froze as it had done before. Dumarest took another slow step forward, another, a third. He dropped as the bird charged.

He fell to his left knee, the sole of his right foot hard against the sand, the leg twisted at right angles to his body. He held the spear low, the butt set into the sand, hard against the side of his right foot. The point slanted upwards, the glimmering tip four feet above the ground and aimed directly at the breast of the charging crell.

He saw it hit, the glimmering steel burying its length into the feathered breast as the running bird impaled itself on the spear. A blow numbed his foot and he saw wood splinter inches from his face as a clawed foot ripped at the shaft in his hands. He released it, feeling the wetness of jetting blood, rolling frantically to one side as the crell tore at the sand, jumping to his feet as the beak stabbed where he had lain.

The roar of the crowd was a thunder to match the pulsing of his blood.

The crell was not dead. Bone had deflected the point from the heart, the pain of the injury driving it into a crazed fury. It saw Dumarest and charged, the butt of the drooping spear hitting the sand and driving the point even deeper. It halted, bewildered, then a clawed foot lifted and tore the spear from its breast.

Dumarest ran forward. He lunged with the full speed of his body, ignoring the pain from his bruised foot in the desperate need of haste. As the crell readied itself to attack with feet and beak he jumped, caught the slender neck and flung his legs over the rounded shape. Beneath him the bird exploded into savage fury, twisting, jumping, reaching up with one leg so as to claw free the thing on its back.

The claws could not reach but the beak could. Dumarest ducked as it struck at his face, gripping the neck with both hands, feeling the tense muscle and sinew, the throb of blood in an artery like a rope. His mouth closed over it, his teeth biting through the tough skin, the gristle beneath, the muscle and flesh—biting until he choked on a sudden gush of blood, a ruby fountain which jetted, glistening into the sunlight.

The rest was a matter of waiting.

It was something she would never forget.

Veruchia sat, bemused by the sound and fury, the blasting release of tension which had risen and was still rising from the stands: men, red-faced, yelling, flinging coins in glittering showers; women, screaming, tearing the clothes from shoulders and chest, offering their bodies to the victor. Emotion was a tangible cloud.

Hysteria, she knew, but knowing did not help. She had attended the games before, seen men die and, rarely, win, but never before had she felt as she did now. She had won. The man she had backed with her wager had won. They had won. They?

She looked at the man on the sand. He was upright, incredibly unhurt, staggering a little as strong arms led him from the arena. He seemed oblivious to the shouts and cheers, the boys collecting the showered offerings, the attendants busy removing the dead crell. How could he know that she had backed him against all logic? How could he guess at the tension which had gripped her stomach as he had fought?

Selkas spoke quietly in her ear. "Look at Montarg. Have you ever seen him look so bitter?"

Her eyes remained on the arena. "He has lost. He hates to lose at anything. Will he pay?"

"He will have no choice. A wager made before witnesses, before Chorzel himself, how can he refuse?" Selkas chuckled with soft amusement. "You should look at him, Veruchia, and enjoy your revenge."

She gave him one glance, seeing the fury, the scowl, then turned away before he could meet her eyes. It was not in her nature to gloat.

"Twelve to one," murmured Selkas. "You played him well. He will be strained to find the money." He chuckled again. "I told you that you could not lose."

"How could you be so certain?"

"I know the man, I told you that. It was on a world whose name I have forgotten, years ago, a little thing but it stuck in my mind. I was bored. A fight had been arranged and I went to see what was offered. It was the usual thing, men set against each other with knives, others gambling on the outcome, a means to pass the time, no more. One of the contestants was young and a little nervous. A handler passed him a knife and, as he reached for it, let it fall. It was caught before it touched the ground." Selkas shrugged. "It is an old trick, one designed to weaken the opposition, a thing arranged so as to reveal a false speed. But this time the accident was genuine. The man was amazingly fast."

She looked at the figure at the far end of the arena. He had almost reached the door; soon he would have vanished from her sight. "That man?"

"The same. I have seen many fighters, so many that their faces are blurred and their skill forgotten, but him I shall never forget. He was young then, new to the ring, far from skilled with a blade, but he was fast. Incredibly so. A matter of reflexes, no doubt, but he was a joy to watch. You noticed how he mounted the crell?"

She nodded.

"That took speed. Speed of decision and action. A fraction of a second's delay and the beast would have turned and torn out his stomach. A lesser man would have hesitated and paid for it with his life. And the rest? Surely you noticed that?"

The racing fury, the charges, the leaping frenzy as the bird died. And even when dead it had continued to thresh about the sand, giant muscles spurred by ungoverned reflexes. Yes, she had noticed.

"I knew that he would win," said Selkas. "A fighter who had managed to survive so long, a man so fast, how could he possibly lose?"

He had gone now, swallowed by the door and, somehow, the arena seemed empty despite the crowd and the men still working on the sand. Veruchia rose, unwilling to watch another bout, knowing that it could only be an anticlimax to what had gone before. And there was no need for her to stay. She had attended the games, Chorzel had seen her; if he protested at her early departure she would plead a sudden indisposition.

She glanced to where he sat, still apparently tense in his chair, his hands clamped on the arms. She sensed an oddity, frowning as she turned, taking three steps before halting to look again. Sweat no longer dewed his face. In a moment she was at his side.

"Quickly," she snapped at the attendants. "Bring something to shade the Owner. Hurry!"

The soggy fabric around his throat resisted her attempts to loosen it and with impatient strength she ripped open the blouse. Beneath he wore a shirt of protective mail and she wondered at his lunacy, sitting in the open sun with such a weight of metal. No wonder he had been so hot.

As the garment yielded to her fingers she snapped, "Summon medical help. Send for his personal physician and bring some ice and water."

Beneath the mail the naked flesh was damp and clammy to her touch, unnaturally cold. Stooping she listened for the heart, at first thinking it had ceased to beat and then catching a faint, turgid echo. She rose and found herself ringed with faces.

Montarg thrust himself forward. "What is wrong?"

"Chorzel is ill."

The Owner? Ill?" Vidda's voice was a strained flutter. "Will he be all right?"

"A stroke, perhaps?" Belev sucked at his teeth. "He was warned against undue excitement."

"Let me see." Izard craned his head. He was echoed by another.

"And me."

"Is he dying?"

They pressed close, predators eager to be in at the kill, still beneath the influence of the arena. Odd, she thought with strange detachment, if the games he had instigated should be the cause of his death.

Sadoua was jubilant. "You did it," he crowed. "You won! Man, I'm proud of you!"

Dumarest straightened. The coolness of the chamber was refreshing after the baking heat outside. He sucked air, filling his chest with deep breaths, oxygenating his blood. A boy came forward with a cup of wine. The fightmaster dashed it from his hand.

"For the winner nothing but the best," he roared. "Bring the iced champagne in the special glasses." He grinned as, his arm heavy around his shoulders, he led Dumarest to a couch. "You'll drink," he said. "And you'll rest. And I'll have the best masseur rub every ache and strain from every inch of your body. Do you know what you've done?"

He snatched the glasses from the boy, handed one to Dumarest and drained his own in a gulp. "You've shown the way to beat the damned birds, that's what. I was watching every second of the time and I can tell when a man calculates his moves and when he's hoping for luck. You knew what you were doing every inch of the way. I guessed it when you made your run and I was sure of it when you moved back. Did you hear the crowd? I thought my ears would burst. Boy! More wine!"

It was cold and sweet and almost evaporated in the mouth.

Dumarest lowered his glass and, as Sadoua refilled it, said, "The money?"

"You'll get it, the tribute too, every coin of it. The boys are collecting it now and they know that I'll have the fingers of any man trying to steal." He lowered his voice a little. "And you can have your choice of a woman too if you want. There isn't a girl or matron out there who wouldn't be proud to take you to her bed. Pay you too. Nothing is too good for a victor."

For a victor, but what if he had lost? Dumarest shrugged. "I can do without the women."

"How about that bitch who yelled for the whip?" urged Sadoua. "You could teach her a lesson. Take a whip to her back and let her know just how it feels. No? Well, have some more wine."

He poured and sat down, his heavy weight depressing the soft padding of the couch.

"You've hunted," he said. "You know how the mind of a beast works. That was a good trick you did with the spear but you aimed a little high. Six inches lower and you'd have speared the heart. You'll know better the next time."

"There won't be a next time."

"No?"

"I was lucky," said Dumarest. "Those spears are too short. If you want to see more men walk from the arena add another foot. And train them. Rig up a dummy crell and teach them how to drop and hold the shaft. And give them a knife." He touched his lips, his teeth. "With a knife I could have sliced that thing's head right off."

"I don't make the rules." Sadoua finished his wine. "But I'll tell you one thing. You'll be back. If you stay on this world you'll have no choice. How else are you going to earn money? And you're good," he complained. "Too good to waste. And it can be a good life. A few fights, money, all the women you can use. A victor gets taken around."

"Like a pet?"

"What's the difference? You'll eat well and live soft. Think about it, huh?"

Dumarest nodded.

"You're always welcome here any time you want a bout." Sadoua lifted his voice. "Larco! Come and do your work."

Dumarest relaxed as the masseur began to rub his limbs. The oil was warm, the man skilled, his probing fingers easing the strain from muscle and sinew. He took his time and Dumarest was almost asleep when he felt the hands leave his body.

"My name is Selkas," said a voice. "Your own, I have been told, is Dumarest. Earl Dumarest. I would like to talk to you."

"Later."

"Now. The matter is of some importance."

Dumarest sighed and opened his eyes. The man was tall and smooth, dressed in rich fabrics, a jeweled chain hanging from his neck. He smiled as Dumarest sat upright and extended his hand, palm flat and upturned.

"A custom of this world," he explained. "I am showing you that I hold no weapon. You are supposed to touch my hand with the palm of your own. It is a gesture of friendship."

"And your other hand?"

"That also." Selkas extended it. "Usually both hands are only displayed to intimates or declared foes if seeking a parley. One in trust, the other to instil confidence. You find the custom amusing?"

"Strange." Dumarest touched the extended hands. The skin was smooth, without trace of thickening, the fingers long and tapered: the hands of an artist, certainly those of a man who had never known physical labor. "And a little pointless."

"Perhaps, but it is very old. Are you interested in ancient things?"

"At times, yes."

"But not at the moment," said Selkas. "Now you want to know why I am here." He glanced around. The couch stood in a secluded corner of the preparation room, the masseur had withdrawn. They stood in a small area of isolation. From outside came a roar and the distant snarl of Sadoua's voice as he cursed the fool who had just spilled his blood on the sand. "The last bout of the day," he mused. "And for someone the last battle of his life. What are your intentions?"

"To take my money and go," said Dumarest.

"To leave this world?" Selkas shrugged. "It could be

done—your pay and tribute would just about buy a High passage—but then what? Arriving destitute on another world? Not a pleasant future, my friend." He reached out and touched the ribs showing clear against Dumarest's chest. "And it would not be wise for you to travel Low. Dangerous, to do it again so soon. You have lost your body-fat and from Dradea journeys are long. It seems that you have little choice but to fight again."

To face the sand, the sun and the savage crell; to hear the roar of the crowd and to pit himself against a beast, trusting always to his own speed and skill. Some thought it a good life but Dumarest knew better. So many things could go wrong: his foot could slip on a patch of buried sand, the shaft of the spear could break, a crell might not blindly follow the expected pattern. On Dradea the odds against the fighters were too high.

Bleakly he said, "There is always an alternative."

"On a strange world with unknown opportunities?" Selkas shrugged. "Perhaps, but I think you know better. You did not fight wholly from choice; necessity must have played its part." Abruptly he said, "I come to offer you employment."

Dumarest had expected it. "Such as?"

"There is a woman who is dear to me for reasons you need not know. A person whom I hold in high regard. I want you to protect her."

"A bodyguard?"

"More than that. I spoke of protection in a wider sense than shielding her from physical attack. She is alone and almost friendless. There are those who have reason to denigrate her and it is important at this time that she appear strong. She needs someone to bolster her courage and determination, a strong man who will be more than a servant. I think you could be that man. Agree and you will have no cause to regret it."

Dumarest said, "Who is this woman?"

"You will see her tonight. I am inviting her to dinner with a few others. You will attend. I shall send for you after dark." Selkas paused and added, "One other thing. I do not want you to let her know I have employed you. You will be invited as a friend. But you will stay close to her, accompany her, insist if she objects. I leave it to you how best to overcome any protest she may make. Do you understand?"

"I think so."

"And you agree?"

"I will tell you that," said Dumarest, "after I have seen the woman."

III

She came running up the stairs, long-legged, lithe, a cloak streaming from her narrow shoulders. At first sight she could have been taken for a boy, a young man still to reach maturity—then Dumarest saw the lips firm yet full, the deep-set eyes of icy blueness, the softness of cheek and throat. He saw too the delicate pattern of ebon over the whiteness beneath, an intricate tracing of darkness as if she had been tattooed in an intricate design. It reached from the collar of her blouse to the roots of her hair, streaks of silver barring the liquid jet which fell rippling like a waterfall almost to her waist.

A wild mutation, the melanine of her skin was concentrated instead of being evenly dispersed. It must spread all over her body so that, naked, she would look as if encased in a spider's web. He saw nothing repulsive about it—the suns of space caused greater distortions than the one she bore—but it was a thing to set any woman apart in a normal society. No wonder the deep-set eyes held the bruised look of someone always on guard.

"Selkas!" She reached out as she came to the head of

the stairs, both arms extended, palms uppermost. "How good of you to invite me."

"You honor my house," he said formally, the palms of his hands touching her own. "Veruchia, allow me to present Earl Dumarest."

"My lady." He repeated Selkas's gesture and caught the expression in her eyes at the unexpected familiarity. A touch of red rose to her cheeks as she dropped her hands. Even her flush was extreme.

She was conscious of it, hating the betraying blood, alarmed at the lack of self-control. The touch of a man's hands, no more, and yet she was reacting like a stupid girl. Vaguely she was aware of Selkas talking as he stood to one side.

"You two have met before," he was saying. "Though I do not expect Earl to remember it. At the time he had other things on his mind. You should thank him, Veruchia, for having won you so much."

So this was the man she had backed in the arena. She stared at him, wondering why recognition had been so long-delayed. The face was somehow different, more relaxed, the hard lines of determination softened a little. And the angle had been deceptive; he was taller than she had guessed, topping her by a head and she by no means short.

"My lady." Dumarest held out his arm. "Is it your wish that I escort you to dinner?"

Again the familiarity. She looked for Selkas but he had gone ahead as if expecting the man to attend her. Well, why not? At least it would be a novel experience. She took the proffered arm and again felt the sudden acceleration of her heart. *A biological reaction caused by the proximity of a male,* she thought bleakly. *How childish can I get?*

"You are new to Dradea?" At least she could make polite conversation.

"Yes, my lady."

"My name is Veruchia. We do not use titles here. Only the Owner. On this world all tenants are equal."

"And the rest, my lady?"

"Veruchia. You mean the landless ones? They too, but there are certain privileges they are denied. Have you fought often?"

"This was the first time."

"On Dradea, of course, I understand." She was pleased that he did not boast or volunteer detail. A lesser man would have bored and sickened her with tales of violence. A lesser man? Why did she set him so high?

Selkas had picked his guests with care. She nodded to Nebka, old and fussing as he took his place. To Wolin and Pezia. Shamar she could have done without and she had no great love for Jebele, but both women held influence. Dumarest, she noticed, had been placed at her side.

"To the Owner!" Selkas lifted his glass in the ritual toast.

"The Owner!"

They drank and the meal commenced, a succession of dishes, spiced, bland, savory, sweet, meat and fish and vegetables cooked and sauced to perfection. Conversation hung like a cloud: the state of the crops, the proposed new harbour, the increase of rent to pay for the games. Nebka spluttered over his wine.

"A waste. A wanton destruction of assets. Oh, yes, I've heard all the arguments and reasons of those who back the arena, but I still say that there must be some other way. You cannot restore the vitality of a race by subjecting it to such disgusting spectacles. Right, Veruchia?"

"You know my feelings on the matter, Nebka."

"The same as mine. Wolin?"

"Are we having a vote?" Wolin touched a napkin to his mouth. "I think we all agree that the cost of the games is far too high. The expense incurred in breeding crells, for example, is increasing all the time. The birds are nonproductive and a continual drag on the economy. If the intention is to stiffen moral fiber why can't men fight against men?"

"Why fight at all?" Shamar leaned across the table, upthrust breasts gleaming above the low neck of her gown. "Personally I find our men virile enough as it is."

"You should know," snapped Jebele spitefully. "You have enough of them."

"Please, ladies." Pezia shook his head then added his contribution. "We must look at the basic claim that we are weak. First, is it true? If it is, what is best done about it? Now I do not personally think that it is true. Weakness is relative and depends much on the prevailing social culture. Any race will have peaks and valleys of achievement and no one is arguing that we are at present in a valley. The birth rate is falling and development has slowed but this state of affairs will not last. It is, if you like, a breathing space. A natural pause. Time will present its own cure without wild experiments such as the games. They are wasteful and, I think, degrading. As I have said often enough before, and all of you have heard me, we should tackle the problem in a more efficient manner."

"Yes," agreed Jebele acidly. "As you say we have heard you often."

"Truth is not diminished by repetition."

"What is truth?" Wolin leaned back in his chair, smiling. "You say one thing, Pezia, the Owner says another. The difference between you is that he has acted while you have not. I agree that the games are wasteful, but what alternative do we offer? Work and build, you say, but how to provide the energy, the will? Our race is sleeping and perhaps Montarg and the others are right. Blood may awaken it and restore its vigor."

Veruchia shook her head. "No."

"How can you be sure?"

"I sense it. People come to the games to watch, not to participate. They want to see violence, not share in it. Not really share." She fell silent, remembering her own recent emotions. Had she simply watched? Or had she been, in part, down on the sand with Dumarest?

She glanced to where he sat beside her and, as if at a clue, Selkas cleared his throat.

"I think we can throw new light on this discussion. We have an expert among us, someone with far greater experience than any of us. What do you think, Earl? You have heard the talk. Do you agree with the contention that blood combat will reenergize the race?"

Dumarest glanced at Veruchia, remembering his instructions, the need to build an affinity between them. But he did not have to pretend.

"No, I do not."

"Would you care to elaborate?" Pezia helped himself to wine. "After all, you have a vested interest in the arena. It seems odd to hear a man decry the means by which he earns a living. Could you give us a little more detail?"

"Go into the arena," said Dumarest tightly. "Fight for your life. Listen to the roar of the crowd and watch as cultured women offer their bodies to a stranger. Smell the stink of blood. That's detail enough. The games breed barbarians."

"But you fight."

"From necessity, not from choice."

Jebele said, "Barbarians. But surely a barbaric culture is a viable one?"

Selkas spoke from where he sat at the head of the table. "For a true barbarian, perhaps, but for civilized people to play at being barbarians is decadance. And a civilized culture plumbs depths of depravity unknown to a genuine primitive. You agree, Earl?"

"Yes, I agree."

Pezia smiled. "You hear that, Wolin? How often have I said it? We are trying to be what we are not. In that lies danger."

"Yet surely there must be something to the mystique of combat?" Shamar displayed a little more of her breasts as she smiled at Dumarest. "You of all people should appreciate that. The spiritual uplift gained by those who watch. The psychological cleansing by the satiation of hidden urges. The wakening of slumbering energies. And it must apply even more to those who actually participate. Don't you feel a rebirth after a bout? A tremendous release? A new determination?"

"No, my lady. I am simply glad that it is over."

"You tease me," she said. "I wish Montarg were here. He could explain it all so much better than I can."

"Has he fought in the arena?"

"Montarg? No, but—"

"Then, with respect, my lady, he is hardly an expert."

She was sharp. "And you are?"

"He is alive," said Selkas quietly. "What more proof do you need?"

The dishes were cleared away and replaced by decanters of spirits, liquers and a variety of tisanes together with tiny cakes crusted with seeds. Dumarest chose a tisane which carried the scent of flowers and held the taste of honey. He sipped it, leaning back, half-listening to the blur of conversation. Casual words tossed back and forth across the table: Montarg, Chorzel and his indisposition, the interplay of opposed factions.

Reaching for one of the tiny cakes he felt the touch of softness as his hand struck another. Like her face it was skeined in black.

"Allow me." He proffered the dish of cakes and looked directly into her eyes.

"Thank you." She made her selection, finding it difficult to look away. Intently she searched his face looking for the old, familiar signs, the tension, the forced politeness, the subtle veil which masked repulsion. They were absent. Incredibly it seemed that this man could look on her as a woman and not as a peculiar monstrosity. For the sake of something to say she said, "You have traveled far?"

"Yes."

"And for long?"

Too long. A forgotten number of worlds and endless reaches of space. Riding High when he could, the magic of quick-time slowing his metabolism so that hours became seconds and months days. "Yes."

"Selkas also." She glanced to the head of the table. "He was away for years when he was young and again after I was born. I think he was bored. Is that why you travel? Because you are bored?"

Deliberately he was casual. "No, Veruchia. I am looking for something. A planet called Earth."

"Earth?" She frowned. "Could a world have such a name? Earth is ground or dirt or soil. It must be a very odd place."

"Not odd. It is old and worn and scarred by ancient wars, but the sky is blue and there is a great, silver moon." He paused and added, "I was born there."

Immediately she understood. "And you want to go back home. That is why you fought in the arena, to gain money for your passage. Well, you won't have to fight again. I won a great deal and some of it is yours. The next time a ship lands we will arrange for it to take you home."

She had the impulsive generosity of a child.

"It isn't that simple, Veruchia." For the first time he used her name. "No one seems to know where Earth lies. They do not have the spatial coordinates."

"But you came from there, you said. Surely you must know the way back."

"I left when I was a boy, scared, stowing away on a strange vessel. The captain was more than kind. He could have evicted me. Instead he allowed me to work my passage. Later he died and I moved on."

Always moving towards the center of the galaxy where suns hung close and worlds were plentiful. Probing deep into regions where the skies were full of glistening sheets and curtains of light. Years of moving until the very name of Earth was a thing unknown.

"You're lost," she said with quick sympathy. "You can't

find your way back. But someone must know where Earth lies. Selkas, perhaps? I'll ask him."

Her voice was clear, sharp as it rose over the blur of conversation. A silence followed the question and Dumarest felt himself tense. He looked down at his hand where it gripped the cup of tisane. His knuckles were white and deliberately he eased his grip. It was stupid to hope and yet hope never died. Perhaps, this time, someone would be able to tell him what he had to know.

"Earth?" Selkas brooded, his eyes sharp beneath his brows. "No, Veruchia, I don't know where it is. I've never been there. But the name is oddly familiar. Earth," he mused. "Earth."

"It has another name," said Dumarest. "Terra. And it lies in this region of the galaxy." That much, at least, he had learned.

"And lost, you say?" Pezia smiled. "How can such a thing be possible? I think, my friend, that you hunt for a legend."

Selkas lifted his head. "A legend! Now I have it! The Original People. They claim to have come from Earth." He smiled. "They claim even more. They state that all men originated on one single world."

"Ridiculous!" Nebka spluttered over his liquer. "The thing is beyond reason. How could all the varied races of mankind have possibly been accommodated on one small planet? I've heard of these people, Selkas. I traveled a little when young and the salon of every ship is a hotbed of rumor and speculation. It is a means of passing the time. Earth is a myth exactly like El Dorado, Jackpot, Bonanza, Eden, a dozen others. Dreams spun out of nothingness."

"Perhaps not." Selkas was thoughtful. "Every legend

holds a grain of fact, a fragment of truth which has become overlaid and buried by a mass of elaboration. It is barely possible that mankind did originate from one point in space. Not a single planet, of course, but a compact region." He stilled the rumble of protest. "Let me illustrate."

His hands moved, tipping the little cakes from their dishes, scattering them thickly towards the center of the table, sparsely towards where he sat.

"Now imagine, for the sake of argument, that mankind originated in an area like this." He pointed to where the cakes were few. "They invented space travel. Yes, I know that it is a thing we have always had with us, but imagine a time when it was new. Mankind headed from their home worlds and where would they have headed? Not towards each other. Certainly not towards the thin edges of the galaxy. They would have aimed their vessels to where worlds without number waited to be exploited." His finger rapped the table where the cakes clustered thickly. "Towards the center."

"And because the planets were close they would have continued to press deeper into the galaxy." Pazia nodded. "You make a good case, Selkas."

Jebele shrugged. "Speculation without proof. An amusing theory, no more."

"But interesting." Wolin frowned at the scattered cakes. "It wouldn't have happened all at once, of course. There would have been a succession of waves as the original worlds revitalized their energies. Diminishing waves, perhaps, until those left lacked the means or will to follow. And time erases memories. The home worlds could have been forgotten or become the fabric of legend." He smiled. "We have one of our own, remember? The First Ship."

"That is no legend!" Veruchia was sharp.

"So you say."

"As I know and so do you all." She stared around the table. "The ship is real, it exists and we know roughly where it is to be found. It is a crime that while fortunes are being wasted it is neglected."

"Calm down, Veruchia." Shamar smiled like a cat as she reached for one of the little cakes. Her teeth gleamed as they bit into it. "What does an old ship matter even assuming that it could ever be found? It's a part of history and, as Wolin says, more a legend than anything else. Something built out of a supposed wreck and a wild hope. Personally I think it a waste of time to dream of the past. You can have it. The present is good enough for me."

Her smile, as she looked at Dumarest, was a naked invitation.

"You claim too much, Veruchia," said Wolin. "We have no proof as to the whereabouts of the ship, assuming that it exists at all. One rumor puts it among the Frenderha Hills, another in the great glacier of Cosne, a third at the bottom of the Elgish Sea."

"Forget the ship," said Shamar. "I'm bored with all this talk of the dead past, old bones and stupid legends. The present is good enough for me. What are your intentions, Earl? Will you fight again or are you interested in other employment? If so it is possible that I may be able to help you to find it." The tip of her tongue wetted the ripe fullness of her lower lip. "Very possible. There is always room in my household for a man with your attributes."

Veruchia said quickly, "He is already engaged."

"Really?" Shamar raised her eyebrows. "In what capacity, my dear?"

Trust the bitch to hit where it hurt! The implication was plain and Veruchia felt herself blush as she invented a duty, praying that Dumarest would not show her up for the fool that she was. And why had she spoken at all? Did it really matter if he took Shamar to bed?

"As my agent. I want him to check the potential of my southern lands."

"And you will pay him well, no doubt." Shamar's smile was loaded with venom. "For your sake, Veruchia, I hope that he does not disappoint you."

"No, my lady," said Dumarest flatly. "I promise that I will not do that."

Veruchia sat back in her chair, relief making her weak. He had not let her down and, more, had played along with the blatant innuendo. At least he had saved her pride.

A servant had entered the chamber during the exchange with a note for Selkas. She saw him read it, dismiss the man with a gesture and rise as the doors closed behind him.

His tone was grave. "Veruchia, we must go to the palace at once. Chorzel is very ill."

He looked dwarfed in the great bed, his giant frame small against the expanse of sheets, defiled by the snaking tubes and mechanisms of the life-support apparatus. Around him the medical attendants stood like green-clad ghosts, silent, waiting. Hamane, white hair awry, face tense, looked up from where he checked a bank of dials. The old doctor was curt: a sure sign of his anxiety.

"He's low, Veruchia. Very low. I doubt if he'll last the night."

"When?"

"He had a relapse a couple of hours ago. The idiot should never have gone to the stadium, I'd warned him often enough to take things easy. He had a minor stroke, nothing too serious in itself, but bad enough for anyone, let alone a man in his condition." Overweight, of course; Chorzel was known for his love of good food and wine. Hamane shook his head. "I got him comfortable and then this happened. It shouldn't and I'm going to find out why. But it did and there's an end to it."

"Is there no hope?"

"None. The brain is affected by massive hemorrhage and he is almost completely paralyzed. He would be dead now but for the mechanisms." His voice softened. "I'm sorry, Veruchia, but these things happen. All things come to an end."

An end to more than a single life. Veruchia crossed to the side of the bed and stood looking down at the helpless shape. It was hard now to imagine him as he had once been: tall and strong and radiating a fierce vitality. She remembered how he had picked her up and thrown her high into the air, grinning at her screams, catching her in his big arms; how he had played with her on too-rare occasions, acting the father she had never known.

But all that had been long ago when she had been a child, before she had grown and they had drifted apart, she into a protective shell and he down odd paths as he pursued misguided theories. Now he was dying and an era was about to end.

She stooped over the bed as she caught the glint of his eyes in the puffed creases of his face. He seemed to want to say something but could only manage a thin drone. She turned away as a nurse wiped the drooling mouth. It was not good to see him so helpless when once he had been so strong.

Selkas had been talking quietly to the doctor. He stepped away to join her, standing before her, his voice low.

"There is nothing more we can do here, Veruchia. Chorzel is as good as dead. He will never speak again and never move. Hamane is certain of it though he will continue monitoring until the last moment."

"Does Montarg know?"

"He was informed but hasn't bothered to attend. I doubt if he will bother and we can both guess why. Already he must be busy making arrangements. Well, we can make our own but we have little time to waste."

"Why bother." The somber atmosphere of the chamber had depressed her. "We know what will happen. Montarg will be accepted and my own claim dismissed."

"Giving up, Veruchia?"

"No." She took a deep breath and squared her shoulders. At least she would make a fight of it. "When are you proposing to summon the Council?"

"At noon tomorrow. Chorzel cannot possibly last that long and so there will be no excuse for delay." His hand tightened on her arm. "This is no time to be weak, girl."

"More advice, Selkas?"

"Was the last so bad?"

"No, but why are you so concerned? You have never shown any great interest before."

"I don't like Montarg. I think he would be bad for this world and that is reason enough for anyone to show concern. It is a time to take sides, Veruchia, and I am taking yours." He urged her from the chamber. "You had better go home now. Dumarest is waiting below, he will attend you."

"I don't need him. I can manage alone."

"Perhaps so, but he needs you, my dear. You employed him, remember?"

She had almost forgotten the stupid gesture. Now, it seemed, she was stuck with it.

"All right," she surrendered. "He can take me home."

She lived in a small house at the edge of the city, a snug place with thick walls and a single floor. The door opened beneath her hand; before she could swing it wide Dumarest had stepped before her, stepping ahead as the door closed behind her. Lights bloomed automatically as they entered the hall and he halted, looking at it. It was warm with carpets on the polished wood of the floor, bright with flowers set in vases of hammered metal.

"You must be tired," she said as he slipped the cloak from her shoulders. "If you're not then I am. It's been a trying day."

He made no motion to leave.

"You have a lovely house, Veruchia. May I look at it?" Without waiting for permission he moved from room to room, walking silently, acting with a deft precision.

She watched him for a moment then entered her study. It was her favorite room, the walls paneled in glowing woods, old maps neatly framed, books lined in neat array. When he joined her she was pouring drinks, golden fluid in goblets of decorated glass.

Handing him one she said, "Well, are you satisfied?"

"With the house?"

"That there is no one lurking in the shadows waiting to attack me."

"If there is I didn't see him." Dumarest sipped at the brandy. "Did you think someone might be?"

"Of course not."

"May I ask how you can be so certain?"

"Dradea is not that kind of a world. Don't judge us by the arena. That is an artificial growth planted by bad advice. The people here are gentle and unused to violence. Chorzel hoped to change that which is why he instigated the games. But you know all this, you heard the talk at dinner and you must have looked around. No, I do not fear personal attack." Her voice became bitter. "And I am hardly in danger of rape."

He knew better than to make the obvious comment. The conviction of a lifetime could not be overcome with a word. Instead he said, casually. "Call it a habit. I like to know my surroundings. I see that you are interested in ancient things."

"The maps? It is a hobby and something more. I have a vested interest in the past." She gestured to a chair. "You may as well finish your drink in comfort. Have you anywhere to stay? Tomorrow I will' arrange for money to be given you. If you haven't enough for tonight something can be arranged."

"I thought it already had. As your agent surely I must remain in your house."

"Impossible! I live alone!"

She caught his smile and realized that she was being stupid, reacting like a scared young girl to imagined dangers. And the reaction had been too strong, too defensive, and she was too intelligent not to know why.

I'm in love with him, she thought bleakly. *In love or*

falling in love and I can't resist it. She fumbled with her brandy, remembering how it had happened before, the young man who had attracted her and who had seemed to find her pleasant—toying with her, holding out the bait of his affection as he would dangle meat before a dog. Then the dreadful realization as he had looked at her and laughed.

She had been fifteen and had never dared to feel tenderness for anyone since that time.

A long time, she thought drearily. Too long. And now it was happening again.

"Veruchia." She felt him close to her and turned to meet his eyes, seeing the strength, the understanding, looking for the pity she dreaded to find. But there was no pity, she was thankful for that. "Veruchia, is anything wrong?"

"No." She turned away and reached for her goblet, the brandy stinging her throat as she gulped it down. "Nothing is wrong. Nothing at all." She drank again and said, "I think you had better go."

"Is that what you want?"

"You know damned well it isn't." She spoke quickly, letting the words flow without restraint. "It's the last thing I want, but for you to stay is the worst thing which could happen. The worst for me. Do you think I could sleep knowing you are in the house? That you are somewhere close while I—" She broke off. "No."

"I shall stay," he said flatly. "I won't bother you. You will bathe and sleep and forget that I am here. But I am not going to leave you alone."

He was too strong for her. Too strong. And then, surrendering, she thought, *why not? Why not do as Shamar*

*had hinted? Why not, just for once, know what it was to
be a real woman?*

If he stayed she would not sleep alone.

The phone rang before she could tell him that. The
soft hum died as he hit the button. Hamane's face
showed on the screen.

"Veruchia," he said. "I am letting everyone know.
Chorzel is dead."

IV

Nothing had changed. Striding into the palace Montarg felt as if he had been cheated. The Owner had ruled so long that it seemed incredible that things should continue as before. Yet the city hummed with life in the morning sun, the subtenants and landless ones indifferent to the events of the previous night. So much for greatness. The ruler of a world died and no one seemed to care.

But he cared and Veruchia would care but then, of course, they had reason.

He mounted the last of the stairs and strode down a passage to where an elevator wafted him high into the building. Chorzel had lived here, loving to stand at his window and see the activity below. He had had the entire section redecorated with barbaric splendor, bright hues and suggestive carvings, shields, swords and helmets set against the walls: a childish extension of his love of the arena.

A scarlet shadow rose before him.

"My lord?"

One of the cyber's acolytes, always on guard, a youth

dedicated to his master's welfare and the organization to which he belonged.

"I am Montarg. Surat is expecting me."

"A moment, my lord." The shadow drifted away and returned silently. "You may enter, my lord."

The cyber occupied a suite of rooms, spartan in their stark simplicity, containing only the essentials of living with no space given to items of luxury. He rose as Montarg entered and stood by his desk, a living flame in the scarlet of his robe, the seal of the Cyclan glittering on his breast. The room was warm despite the conditioning and Surat had thrown back the cowl of his robe. In the light streaming through the windows his shaven head had the appearance of a skull.

"My lord." He bowed, waiting.

Montarg said, "Congratulations, cyber, your prediction was one hundred percent correct. The Owner is dead."

"An easy prediction to make, my lord."

"True, all men must die, but you stated the very hour of his passing."

"A matter of simple extrapolation, my lord." The cyber's voice was an even modulation devoid of any irritating factor. "I knew his physical condition and I had information from the life-support apparatus to which he was attached. To predict his death was a thing any acolyte could do with as great an accuracy. I trust the prediction was of value?"

"It gained me time, cyber. I must thank you for that."

"And now, my lord?"

"Hamane is suspicious He insists on conducting an investigation into the Owner's death. What will be found?"

"The prediction that he will discover traces of assassination is of a probability factor of sixty-eight point seven. He will be swayed by his own inability to account for the unexpected relapse and eager to shift the blame. The evidence will be insufficient to convince others."

Montarg nodded, relieved. "There is little doubt that I shall inherit. The question now is are you willing to serve me as you did Chorzel?"

"I serve the Cyclan, my lord. If you wish to engage their services it could no doubt be arranged. Would your policy be the same?"

"I don't know. I must think about it. Chorzel had some good ideas but I'm not sure that he operated with the highest possible efficiency." His tone sharpened a little. "I hold you to blame for that, cyber. He relied on your services a little too much. A man should make his own decisions."

"I advise, my lord, nothing more. I do not judge, condemn or take sides. My duties lie in offering you the logical outcome of any proposed course of action, to help you arrive at a decision by presenting you with the inevitable result of any sequence of events."

To take a handful of facts and from them to extrapolate a hundred more. To take what was and to predict what must inevitably be. A living computer with a machine for a brain.

"Power," said Montarg slowly. "Chorzel wanted power. But he owned a world, what greater power could a man have?"

"What is power, my lord? Wealth? Money can only buy the things which are available. Force? Always there is the danger that a greater force may arise to crush your own. Influence? That is determined by the shift of circumstance. True power lies in only one thing: the ability to make others do as you dictate. Once achieve that and the rest will follow. But a civilized man is rarely loyal in the truest sense of the word. His mind is diversified, his energies unchanneled, lost in a web of opposed ideals. The late Owner knew that."

Montarg knew it too well He remembered the long talks, the theories, the empty yearning in Chorzel's voice when he had spoken of other cultures: how a thousand men had willingly died at their ruler's word; how old chieftains had been buried with a hundred warriors who had slain themselves in order to follow their leader into death. Loyalty of such a nature was rare.

"He wanted to be a king in the truest sense," he said. "To sit on his throne and know that he had the world at his feet."

"And you, my lord?"

The temptation was irresistible: to sit in the high box at the arena, to occupy the royal seat and to hold ultimate rule. He remembered the roar of the crowd and imagined what it would be like for them to roar, not at the spectacle of death, but at the sight of his living presence. To own a world, not of tenants and landless ones, but of slaves.

He blinked, conscious of the cyber's watching eyes, aware that his imagination had been led down selected paths. But still the temptation remained.

"We must discuss this once I have inherited. What is your prediction as to that?"

"The probability that the Council will recognize your claim is eighty nine percent."

"It should be a hundred."

"That would be certainty, my lord, and nothing can be certain. Always there is the possibility of an unknown factor and any prediction must allow for that. And I must warn you that my prediction is based on my present knowledge as to the situation. If there is anything you know which could affect it you would be wise to keep me informed"

Montarg glanced at the papers neatly piled on the desk, a mass of reports and associated data, trivia some of it, but every scrap holding meaning to the cyber.

Dryly he said, "Your own sources of information seem adequate."

"There is a time-lag, my lord, impossible to avoid. An event could be taking place at this very second which would completely alter the value of my prediction. An assassin waiting to kill you, for example. If he was successful how could you inherit?"

"You suspect that?"

"The order of probability is very low, but still it exists and must be taken into account. Therefore, my lord, if you have any information of recent origin, do not hesitate to let me know."

"Selkas has been unusually active." Montarg glowered. "Who would have guessed that he would take such an interest? Episko could not be found, his servants said that he was on a hunt, and Boghara has demanded a promise that, if I inherit, I will close the arena. And Veruchia has a lover," he added as an afterthought. "A fighter from the arena."

"A lover, my lord?"

"Incredible, isn't it? A day ago you would have predicted it an impossibility. Anyone would who knew her. But the fact remains, I have the news from those who saw them together, and there can be no doubt. They said she was acting like a stupid girl. Probably paying him off for having won her so much money." His face darkened at the memory. "Dumarest," he said. "Earl Dumarest. I shall remember that name."

"It would not be wise to pursue what you have in mind, my lord."

"Why not? Veruchia made me look a fool and to rob her of her lover would be a sweet revenge."

"He is a trained fighter. You could hire assassins but they could fail and they could be made to talk. I must emphasize the delicacy of any predictions I may make at this time, my lord. Small events can have farreaching consequences and could easily upset the present pattern. Perhaps you would be interested in studying certain extrapolations I have made based on varying courses of action suggested by the late Owner. They may serve as a guide to your own decisions."

Later, when Montarg left the cyber's chamber, he halted before the barbaric decorations, his head swimming with golden concepts. Chorzel had been more devious than he'd guessed; the future prospects as displayed by Surat were intoxicating in their promise.

He let his eyes drift over the shields, the swords, helmets and spears, the suggestive carvings. Now they did not seem as childish as they had before.

Alone Surat stood for a long moment beside his desk and then, sitting, allowed his mind to integrate the recently aquired data. Montarg was no problem; the man was like a child easily bribed with bright toys, unable to see the hand offering the bait. He could be swayed and influenced and led in the path the Cyclan wished him to take. When he became the Owner he would have all the trappings of rule but the real power would reside, as always, with the organization of which Surat was a part.

He pressed a button and, as an acolyte entered the room, said, "A man fought in the arena, yesterday. His name is Dumarest. Obtain all available information."

The young man bowed. "Yes, master."

"At once. The matter is urgent."

He returned to the papers on his desk, scanning them with trained speed, assimilating a thousand items of information, his brain, even as he read, correlating them into a whole. Crops had failed in the Tien province, a tidal wave had destroyed a village on the coast, fissures had been seen at a point far to the south. In the city a man had been murdered, apparently attacked without reason and his body viciously hacked with knives. Two new shops had opened dealing in the sale of defensive clothing. A proposal stood before the Council for the construction of a larger arena. Attrition among those taking higher education had once again shown a marked increase. The police were demanding greater mobility and higher pay.

The communicator hummed and he pressed the button. It was the acolyte making his report.

"Master, the man Dumarest arrived on Dradea five days ago. He had little credit and used it all to pay for lodgings and a high-protein diet. Apparently unable to obtain suitable employment he volunteered to fight in the arena. At present he resides in the home of High Tenant Veruchia."

"He is to be kept under surveillance. Attend to it."

"Master."

The young face, already hard in its determination, vanished as Surat broke the connection. Another, almost its twin, met Surat's eyes as he entered his inner room.

"Maximum seal," he ordered. Even command did not

harden the soft tones of his voice, but there was no need for aural emphasis. "No interruption of any nature is to be permitted."

As the acolyte left to stand guard at the closed door of the chamber, Surat touched the thick bracelet locked around his left wrist. Invisible forces flowed from the mechanism to set up a field which no spying device could penetrate.

Lying supine on the narrow bed he closed his eyes and concentrated on the Samatchazi formulae. His heartbeat slowed, his breathing became shallow, his temperature dropped as if he were asleep. Gradually he lost all sense of feeling; had he opened his eyes he would have been blind. He rested, detached, unstimulated by external reality, only his individual awareness locked within his skull remaining alive. Only then did the grafted Homochon elements become active.

Surat entered another world

It was a place of shifting rainbows, a wonderous kaleidoscope of varying colors, crystalline, splintering into new and entrancing formations. He seemed to move through a maze of brilliance, shafts and spears and arching lines of the purest color reaching endlessly to all sides. Planes shifted and he caught glimpses of unguessable truths, all the mysteries of the universe trembling at the edge of discovery. And the colors were alive, throbbing with intelligence and personal awareness. He was one with them, of them, sharing and giving in a universal gestalt, feeling his ego expand even as it was taken and used to expand that of others.

And somewhere towards the center of that dazzling complex of light was the pulsing heart and brain of the Cyclan. Buried deep beneath miles of rock the central intelligence was the nexus from which flowed the tremendous power which spanned worlds. It touched his mental presence and absorbed his knowledge as light swallows darkness. There was nothing as slow as verbal communication, only a mental communion in the form of words—instantaneous, organic transmission against which the speed of supra-radio was the merest crawl.

"Dumarest! On Dradea?"

Affirmation.

"Incredible that previous predictions could have been so incorrect. There is no possibility of doubt?"

Negation

"The possibility of error remains. Until it is resolved give him your full attention. The importance of this man cannot be overemphasized. All care must be taken. Keep me informed."

Agreement

"Accelerate plans as regards new Owner. Time permitted for fulfillment reduced by one-quarter."

A question.

"Under no circumstances. You will be held personally responsible."

That was all.

The rest was an ecstasy of mental intoxication, the nearest thing to sensual pleasure a cyber could ever know.

Always after rapport, during the time when the grafted Homochon elements sank back into quiescence and the machinery of the body began to reassociate itself with the mind, came this period of supreme revelation. Surat drifted in an endless limbo while he sensed alien memories and unremembered situations, caught flashes of eerie thought, experienced strange environments: scraps of overflow from other minds, the residue of powerful intelligences, caught and transmitted by the power of central intelligence, the vast cybernetic complex which was the power of the Cyclan.

One day he would become a part of it.

He rose to full awareness, opening his eyes and looking at the sunlight painting bright patterns on the ceiling of his chamber, tracing in the symmetry of light and shadow the lines of his own future. His body would age and die but his brain would be salvaged, taken and incorporated into the body of central intelligence, there to remain living and aware until the end of time. He would become a part of a superior being, a massed complex of living brains, sharing and experiencing always the gestalt he had just experienced.

His reward. The reward of every cyber if they obeyed and did not fail.

She was young and lithe and full of passion. She had come to him with a burning intensity, throwing aside all restraint. In the darkness the skein of ebon she wore had been invisible; in the daylight he saw only that it added to her beauty.

"Lover!" She clung to him as water gushed over their heads, sharing her shower as he had shared everything else. "Earl, you wonderful, wonderful man!"

She snuggled against him as his hand stroked the barred mane of her hair. Her finger traced the thin cicatrices on his torso.

"You're marked too. We've a lot in common."

"Does it bother you?" He smiled down into her upturned face, liking the way she screwed up her eyes against the impact of the water.

"That you're scarred? Of course not." She lowered her face, her voice muffled against his chest. "Earl, it wasn't just a hunger? I mean, you didn't stay with me because I was just a woman?"

"No."

"I believe you," she said. "I want to believe you. But more than that I want the truth. You don't have to be afraid to tell me. I'd rather know than guess and, well, men do these things, don't they? Have casual relationships, I mean. Have you?"

"Yes, but this wasn't one of those times."

"You knew that I wanted you to say that." She turned off the water and they felt the warm blast of scented air drying their skins. "You're kind, Earl, and gentle and wonderfully understanding. I suppose you think I'm talking and acting like a fool. Well, maybe I am, but it was the first time and I've never felt like this before."

Happy, she thought. *This must be what is meant by happiness. To feel all soft and romantic and really alive. A woman in love and who is loved in return. If he did love her. If he hadn't just used her.* Firmly she shook her head. Such thoughts were destructive and had no place now.

She reached up and wound her arms around his neck, pressing herself close as she kissed him on the lips. If this were madness then let it rule. The hum of the phone seemed to come from a great distance.

"Damn!" She wanted to let it ring but the tone was imperious. "I'd better answer it, it could be important. Don't vanish now. Promise?"

Dumarest smiled as she ran from the shower. Dried, he began to dress, adjusting the tunic as she returned.

"It was Selkas, he's coming right over." Naked, she

closed the distance between them. "I don't know what he's going to think when he sees you here. He'll probably call me all kinds of a bitch and not want to see me again."

"No," said Dumarest. "He won't do that."

"I don't suppose that he will. I don't think I could shock him if I tried." Stretching, she looked down at herself. "You know, if anyone had told me yesterday that I would be standing like this in front of a man I would have called him a liar. But it seems so natural. Earl?"

"You had better get dressed."

"But, Earl—"

"And you had better do it fast." He had caught the tension in her voice.

"Yes." She bit at her lip, conscious that she had trodden the edge of danger. Almost she had demanded the reassurance of his love. "Yes, I suppose I had. Selkas will be here soon and there's a lot to do before we go to the Council meeting. Have some breakfast if you want. Don't bother to cook anything for me, I'm too excited to eat."

"You'll eat."

"Bullying me, Earl?"

"Advising. An empty stomach is no one's friend. Eat while you have the chance." He smiled. "That is traveler's philosophy, a good rule to live by when you can never be sure where the next meal is coming from. Now get dressed while I cook some food."

Selkas arrived as he was clearing the dishes. He followed Dumarest into the kitchen and watched as he disposed of the soiled containers. "Veruchia?"

"In the study. Alone."

"Good, she has much to do and little time in which to

do it." Selkas helped himself to a cup of tisane. "Have you anything to report?"

Dumarest shook his head. She had sat quietly for a while after Hamane had phoned and then had gone into her study. Later, after he thought her asleep, she had come to him. He remembered her initial tension, the way she had clung to him as if seeking strength. A woman afraid, needing to restore her self-confidence.

"Good." Selkas sipped at the tisane. "A man of many achievements," he mused. "You fight, you cook and you can act the servant. And it seems that you have a great attraction for women. Shamar called me early this morning. She wanted to know if I would use my influence to pursuade you to enter her household. Naturally I told her that you were not available. However I suspect that the main reason she called was to let me know it is common knowledge that you stayed here the night."

"You object?"

"Certainly not. Veruchia can do as she pleases. In fact I must congratulate you on the skillful execution of your duties. How else could you take care of her should the need arise? But if she told me then she has told others. You must take extra care to protect her."

"Protect her from what?" Dumarest looked at the modest appointments of the kitchen. "A woman alone, of no great means and no apparent position, who could possibly want to harm her?"

Selkas raised his eyebrows. "You don't know? She hasn't told you?"

"No. I can understand how she could be hurt by sadistic comments, but any bravo could take care of that. You promised me high pay and I assume you had a reason. But I fail to see it."

"There are two heirs to a fortune and one is ambitious. Is that reason enough?"

"Perhaps, if the fortune is large enough. And if the ambitious one is sure to get the other's legacy. Is it large?"

"Very large." Selkas set down his cup, he had hardly touched the tisane. "The entire world, in fact. Veruchia stands to inherit the whole of Dradea."

They glided high over the city, the raft steady in the still air, a sprawling mass of streets and houses, business premises, factories, the open mouth of the arena like a gaping sore. Beyond lay neat farms and rolling countryside, hills looming on the horizon. A nice world with tremendous possibilities and she stood to gain it all.

Dumarest watched her as she sat against the cushions. She had changed, closing in on herself, her face a mask of cold determination. No wonder that she had needed strength. He hoped that he had given it to her.

"We shall be late," said Selkas. "Never mind. We can afford to be a little impolite for the sake of a good entrance."

Others had the same idea. A raft landed seconds after their own and Montarg came towards them. He was smiling.

"Veruchia, my dear, how good to see you. You are looking well. The medicine you took last night seems to agree with you. You should take more."

Selkas said, "Enough, Montarg."

"You find the truth unpleasant? Well, that cannot be helped. I am pleased that Veruchia has followed my advice and taken a man to her bed. She was lucky to have found one willing to cooperate. However, there is no accounting for taste."

Dumarest stepped forward. "You will apologize. At once."

"Apologize? To you?"

"To the lady Veruchia."

"And if I do not?" Montarg's eyes reflected his rage.

"You have regular features. It would be a pity to spoil them, but if you do not apologize I shall see the color of your blood."

Selkas said, "He means that he will break your nose, Montarg. I am sure that he will do it. I should apologize if I were you. After all, the remark was in very bad taste."

"You ask the new Owner to apologize to a dog from the arena?"

"You aren't that yet, Montarg. And the apology is to Veruchia, not Dumarest."

He was not going to apologize. Dumarest could tell it and he moved a little closer as Montarg's fingers twitched at his sleeve. At the first sight of a weapon he would act, one hand gripping the wrist, the other striking at the throat.

"Never mind, Earl." Veruchia laid her hand on his arm. "I am used to Montarg's pleasantries. And this is no time to quarrel, the Council is waiting."

They sat at a long table, the High Tenants of Dradea, men and women both, all solemn as befitted the occasion. Dumarest watched them as he took his place in the gallery. Next to him a plump merchant sucked at a sweetmeat with liquid enjoyment.

"This is the biggest thing I've seen," he whispered. "Chorzel ruled so long that I never thought it would ever happen. Are you interested in politics?"

"I thought this was just a formality."

91

"It should be. A man dies and his heir inherits, but it isn't as simple as that. Chorzel had no children and it is up to the Council to decide which aspirant has the better claim." He shoved another sweet into his mouth. "Are you a betting man?"

Dumarest smiled. "I've been known to gamble."

"I'll give you two to one on Montarg. Is it a bet?"

"Do you think he'll win?"

"I hope not, but I'm afraid he will." The plump man craned forward over the rail as an usher called for silence. "Well, here we go."

Andreas was the Chairman. He stood, old and dressed in somber fabrics, his dry voice rustling through the chamber.

"This meeting of the Council was summoned by Selkas. Are there any objections?"

It was ritual; no one could possibly object.

"Chorzel is dead. Dradea is without an Owner. The custody of the planet resides with the Council until we determine the lawful heir."

A man said, "There is no doubt as to his death?"

More ritual, but the correct procedures had to be followed.

"None. The physician Hamane and three others have signed sworn testimony and the corpse has been viewed by seven members of this assembly. Their statements and names are on record." He paused and took a sip of water. "We are faced with an unprecedented situation. Chorzel died childless. He was the eldest of three brothers and inherited in the normal manner. The other two brothers, twins, each had one child, Veruchia and Montarg. Each lays claim to the inheritance."

Lounging in her chair at the foot of the long table Shamar said, "Surely one must have the greater right?"

"That is what we are here to determine. Montarg?"

He rose, tall and arrogant, jewels making bright glimmers on fingers and throat. He said, "As my father and that of Veruchia were twins the question of precedence does not arise. However I am older than she by a year and so have the greater claim."

"Veruchia?"

"Admitting that Montarg is the eldest I still have the greater right. My mother was in direct line of descent from the First Owner."

"That is a lie!"

"Montarg!" Andreas slammed his hand on the table. "How dare you raise your voice in Council?"

"It is still a lie. Lisa was of the family Chron. Everyone knows that the name of the First Owner was Dikarn." His shrug was contemptuous. "It shows how weak is her claim that she has to rely on a thing so false."

"Not so." Pezia rose to his feet. "Chron was the First Owner. If her mother was in direct descent then she has made her case. Veruchia should be the next Owner of Dradea."

"Dikarn was the First!"

"No, Chron!"

Dumarest heard the plump man give a soft whistle as a storm rose in the chamber. "Well, this beats the arena hands down. Wait until I tell the wife! See Montarg? If looks could kill Veruchia would be dead. What a battle!"

"I don't understand. What's it all about?"

"It's an old argument, but I never thought it would come to this. When the First Ship landed the owner, naturally, claimed the planet as his own property. Most think that his name was Dikarn and every Owner since then has claimed the right by direct descent. Fair enough, but there is a strong rumor that Dikarn wasn't the true owner at all but that Chron was the real claimant. It hasn't mattered up till now because no one has been in a strong enough position to argue. If Chorzel had had a child, for example, this couldn't have happened. But he didn't and Montarg and Veruchia are running neck and neck. He is the oldest, but a lot of people would rather see Veruchia inherit. With things so close they're doing their best to see she does."

"Do you think she will?"

"I doubt it. Montarg has the edge. They may not like him but they can't dismiss his claim. And you know how it is, there are always those ready to back the winning side." He grunted as the clamor died. "I hope she wins."

Andreas rose from his seat at the head of the table. He was shaking with anger and his voice echoed his disgust.

"In all my years as Chairman I have never seen such a spectacle as I have been forced to witness. You are the High Tenants of Dradea and, at this time, the custodians of the welfare of this world. The matter we have to determine is too grave to permit such emotional behavior."

Montarg snapped, "We can do without your speeches. I demand that my claim be recognized."

"Montarg forgets himself." Selkas rose, his voice silky. "He is not yet the Owner and I will be frank, I hope that he never is. His conduct at this assembly has left much to be desired. On the other hand Veruchia has shown herself capable of restraint under extreme provocation. As she can claim direct descent from the First Owner of her mother's side then I suggest that we allow her to inherit."

He glanced around the table. Now? There would never be a better time. "Shall we put it to the vote?"

"I protest!" Montarg was quick to recognize the danger. "Selkas is playing on the emotions of those present. The inheritance is not decided on the basis of popularity but of fact. I have the facts on my side. I am the eldest. I should inherit."

"But if her mother was descended from Chron then she has the right."

Montarg sneered. "If? Have you any proof that Chron is more than a legend? Are we to give value to folklore?"

"I can prove it," said Veruchia. "Give me time and I will."

Andreas relaxed. He had been tense, afraid of putting matters to the vote, knowing that unless the Council were of a mind any such decision could only lead to later trouble. Once before, a century ago, there had almost been civil war. Then a younger brother had collected a cabal and only the swift employment of an assassin had prevented the danger. But the girl had shown him the way out.

"We are heated," he said, and, with a sharp glance at Montarg, "I do not intend to make a speech. However, in all fairness to both aspirants and for the good of Dradea I announce that this assembly be adjourned for a period of one hundred days. Unless Veruchia can provide proof that she is in direct line of the First Owner then Montarg will inherit." His hand fell heavily on the table. "This session is over."

Selkas said, "Things have turned out badly, Earl. Now, more than before, Veruchia needs protection."

"You fear assassination?" Dumarest glanced at the

closed door of the study. She had remained silent all the way home, running into her room as soon as they arrived. *To cry,* he thought, *to find release in the woman's anodyne of tears.* "Montarg? Two can play at that game."

"It wouldn't do any good. Montarg has a child and he would inherit."

"Would the Council allow it if Veruchia was to die?"

"They would have little choice. She must be kept close and watched at all times. It would be better if she were to go off-world. Would you travel with her, Earl?"

"There's nothing to hold me on Dradea."

"No, I suppose not. Well, let us see if she agrees."

She hadn't been crying. She sat at her desk behind a litter of papers, frowning as she studied graphs and writings. "Selkas, help yourself to brandy. You too, Earl." She accepted the glass he placed in her hand. "A hundred days. It isn't long."

"It will pass." Selkas looked at the papers. "Tidying up, Veruchia? It is just as well. There's no point in leaving loose ends around when you leave."

"Leave?"

"I think it best that you take passage to some other world."

"Why?"

"You can't inherit. I know that many of the Council are with you but Montarg still has the right on his side. I had hoped that your own claim would receive greater acceptance, but you saw how things went. Andreas did the best he could but a hundred days is the maximum period the Council can delay. Montarg will be the new Owner at the end of that time."

"I'm not leaving," she said. "And Montarg will not inherit. Not if I can find the necessary proof."

"Does it exist?"

"Maybe not," she admitted. "But I feel sure that it does. All we have to do is to find it."

Selkas frowned. "Where?"

"In the First Ship."

He made a soft noise, something between a grunt and a sigh, a sound composed of disbelief and pity. "Veruchia, are you serious? Do you honestly expect to locate and excavate that old vessel? If it exists at all. Girl, the thing is beyond all reason."

"You talk without thinking, Selkas. We settled this world, correct? We must have come here in a ship, correct? That ship is said to still remain on Dradea, correct? Right, now give me one good reason why we can't find it?"

"Because it's lost. Because no one knows where it could be."

Dumarest said, "If it wasn't lost there would be no need to find it."

Selkas ignored the comment. Setting down his glass he began to pace the floor, his face concerned. "Veruchia, this is madness. Aside from anything else you haven't the time to search this planet for a thing so small. And, for another, you haven't the money."

"I will have when Montarg pays what he owes. And you misjudge me. I've been working on this for years. I've a good idea where the ship is to be found." Paper rustled as she jerked maps from a drawer and threw them on the desk. They were covered with little marks, crosses and checks in red and black, circles and squares. "These are places I've checked in the past. Old settlements, mostly, some deposits of rubbish and a few discarded workings. This is a mass of iron ore and this an underground stream. I tried to retrace the progress of the original settlers. We know there was a city to the north which is now covered with ice. The climate is constantly altering and there was, and is, considerable volcanic activity."

"Well?"

"Let us imagine what must have happened. The First Ship landed and we know there was trouble at that time. The settlers would have had to take steps to survive, choose a place to build and so on. After a generation or so the ship would have lost its importance. Then, maybe, something happened, an earthquake, perhaps. The people had to move and start again. After a while they would have forgotten the location of the ship. How long does it take, Selkas, for memories to fade? Three hundred years, five, a thousand?"

She looked at Dumarest as he made no comment.

"What do you think, Earl? You've lost a planet—is it so strange that a planet could lose a ship?"

"No, Veruchia."

"I can find it," she said. "I know that I can and in it will be the proof I need to prove my right to inherit this world."

"You can't be sure of that, Veruchia." Selkas halted his pacing. "I think you're clinging to a dream. You could squander a fortune and end with nothing."

"Earl?" She stepped from behind the desk and came towards him, halting, lifting her hands to rest on his chest. "Advise me, Earl. You spend your life searching for a forgotten world. I want to spend a hundred days looking for a ship. You gamble your life for a little money. I want to spend a little money in order to win an entire planet. Am I so wrong?"

The odds were right and he had gambled too often for some of the lure not to have entered his blood. Yet it was not for him to guide her decision.

"You must do as you think best, Veruchia."

"I do what I must." If she were disappointed at his lack of support she didn't show it. "I don't think Montarg will be good for this world and I don't think any decent person will want to see what he does with it. Perhaps I can prevent that, at least I must try. Will you help me, Selkas?"

His urbanity had returned. Smiling he picked up his brandy. "How can I refuse? I'll see that Montarg pays what he owes and do anything else you require."

"And you, Earl?"

Her eyes were pleading, hurt dimming their brightness as he hesitated. Womanlike she could only think of one reason for his slowness.

"I'm sorry. It seems that I ask too much."

"It isn't that. I hadn't intended to stay long on Dradea and I should be on my way."

Taking ship, moving on to some other world to earn the price of a passage, moving again in order to lose himself among the stars and to continue his search for the world he needed to find. But she would never be able to understand. He saw the movement of her hand as it rose as if to touch her face, then lowered with conscious effort.

"Veruchia." He caught the hand and pressed it, the strength of his fingers hard against the flesh. "Come with me. Do as Selkas advises. There are a thousand worlds on which to find happiness."

"Earl!" For a moment she wavered and then, blinking at the smarting of her eyes, firmly shook her head. "You will never know what it meant to me to hear you say that. But I can't, Earl. Not yet. Not until I have tried to find the First Ship. A world, Earl. An entire planet for us to share if I win and a hundred days lost if I lose." Then quietly, she added, "It is a very old vessel, Earl. Very old. Who knows what it may contain? Something to help you, perhaps. Information on the place you seek."

Navigational tables, ancient and with coordinates based on a different system to that now used; the center of the galaxy could not always have been the determining point. Tables carried, if legend held truth, long ago when men had first reached for the stars: such tables would show him exactly where Earth was to be found.

It was a gamble but one he had to take. Like Veruchia he had nothing to lose.

V

Against the sky the raft was a black mote topped with a glistening bubble, the rays of the setting sun turning the transparency into a glowing ruby. Dumarest watched it as it almost vanished from sight, seeing it turn, realign and grow as it came towards him. Three times he watched as it traversed the area and then, cold beginning to penetrate his clothing, he turned and entered the hut.

Inside it was warm and bright with glowing tubes. Veruchia looked up from where she sat at a table poring over her maps and associated data.

"Has it landed yet, Earl?"

"Not yet."

"Why do they take so long?" She was, he noticed, beginning to show the strain. Weeks of intense effort had edged her temper and thinned her face. "If they increased the speed they could cover the area that much faster. We haven't time to take things easy."

"Izane knows what he's doing." Dumarest looked over her shoulder at the sheets on the table. A contour map of the region was covered with a mass of tiny marks, some in clusters, most widely scattered. "Is this the preliminary scan?"

"Yes." She watched his face. "All right, you don't have to say it. I'm wasting my time."

"I didn't say that."

"But you thought it. You all think it. Earl, am I being a fool?"

"No, just impatient."

"For success, yes." Her hand slapped at the papers. "I was so sure the ship would be found in this region. I would have gambled on it. Centuries ago this was a warm area and a logical place to have founded an early settlement. The weather changed. The cold would have driven them further south towards where the city is now. The ship, left behind, would have become buried with snow. The snow would have turned to ice. Logical, isn't it?"

It was more logical that those who had arrived in the ship would have torn it apart for needed materials, but he didn't say that. Legend claimed that the vessel had become a shrine, an object of veneration, but who could trust legend? Facts became distorted over the passage of years.

"You're tired," he said. "You should sleep."

"Later. Hasn't Izane landed yet?"

"He will report when he does." Dumarest studied the map again. The raft held an electronic device which sent pulses into the ground. Reflected they revealed any distortion in the material below. With careful calculation both the nature and size of any buried object could be determined. "Did they check on that object found at Wend?"

A second raft had reported a find.

"It was a subterranean storage compartment. Empty, waterlogged and about three hundred years old. It was the only possibility we found. I've sent the raft over to the Elgish Sea."

"The site you decided was the lowest in order of probability?"

"Yes." She looked at him curiously. "That's an odd way to put it. If I didn't know better I'd think you were a cyber. That's the way they talk, always so carefully precise. You've met cybers?" .

"Yes," he said bitterly. "Too often."

"And you don't like them?"

"I've no reason to love them. Is there one on Dradea?"

"Surat. He lives in the palace and used to advise Chorzel. I suppose he advises Montarg now. I saw him a couple of times when I was working on my maps. I asked him to help me determine where the First Ship could be lying and he picked Wend and the Elgish Sea. I remember that he said the sea was lowest in order of probability." She shivered. "An odd person. He gave me the creeps. He looked at me exactly as if I were an interesting specimen."

Which, to him, was exactly what she was. No cyber could ever feel emotion; an operation on the thalmus performed at puberty had made that impossible. They moved through life as living, thinking machines, utterly incapable of experiencing love and hate, hope and fear, their only pleasure the mental gratification of making successful predictions.

"Is something wrong, Earl?"

"Nothing." He had been lost in thought. A cyber on Dradea: it was to be expected and it was certain that the man knew of his presence on this world. He should have left after the fight in the arena. Now it was too late.

"There is something wrong." She rose, immediately concerned. "You're worried, Earl. Is it about the cyber? Does the Cyclan threaten you in any way?"

"I have something they want, that's all." He forced himself to smile. "Forget it. They can't hurt me here and, once you find the ship, I'll have your full protection." He cocked his head at the soft crunch of feet. "Here's Izane."

He was a short man of middle age, his hair gray and his face impassive. A lifetime spent with electronic devices had taught him the value of patience and determination. He set a sheaf of papers on the table.

"Anything?" Veruchia couldn't wait. "Did you find the ship?"

"We found two possibilities." He selected a sheet and rested his finger on the mass of flecks. "Here and here. The first is buried about two hundred feet below the surface, the second about half that. You realize, of course, that this is just a secondary survey and the objects could be anything. My guess is that they are accumulations of rock compressed beneath the ice."

"But you can't be sure?"

"As yet, no," he admitted. "Tomorrow I will make a more precise scan of both areas using equipment more finely calibrated for the discovery of metal."

"Tomorrow?"

"It is getting late and the temperature is falling. By the time we leave it would be dark."

"That doesn't matter," said Dumarest. "We have lights and the cold won't bother us in the raft. We'll leave as soon as you have adjusted your equipment." His tone sharpened as Izane hesitated. "Get on with it, man. If we find anything we can have a crew out there by dawn ready to start excavations. Veruchia, you had better put on some warmer clothing."

The technician frowned. "You are coming with us? The raft will not hold both you and the regular crew."

"I can handle a raft," said Dumarest. Anything was better than more of the empty waiting. "Leave a couple of men behind. You can check the apparatus and Veruchia will be able to decide what has to be done. Hurry now."

It was dark when they left. Dumarest sent the raft lifting high and fast towards the position Izane had marked. Beyond the canopy the stars glittered with an icy brightness, the blobs of nebulae showing like patches of glimmering mist. Below the ice caught the starlight and reflected it in a milky sheen. As he neared the selected point he switched on the searchlights and illuminated the area. The light was strong, penetrating; in its beam he could see vague shapes buried deep in the ice. The ship could be one of them.

"Rubbish," said Izane as he stood beside his machine. "Masses of accumulated detritus, trees, rocks, natural objects caught and buried over the course of years. The deeper they are the older they will be. Slow down now, please. Jarg, I think you had better take over." He looked at Dumarest as his assistant sat at the controls. "No disrespect, but he is far more experienced in this work. It is important that we maintain a constant elevation. If you will stand by the feedout you can stack the record sheets as they emerge." He pressed buttons and the screen of his apparatus flared to life. "In position, Jarg? Good. Now let us see what lies below."

Veruchia looked at the dancing motes on the screen. "Is this the preliminary scan?"

"Yes. Before trying to get greater definition I must determine that we are at the correct point. Minimum velocity, Jarg. A little to the right. Hold!" He made a series of adjustments. "There, you can see it quite clearly now."

It was an irregular mass about three times as long as it was wide, a crumpled shape which defied recognition. A ship? Dumarest doubted it though it was barely possible. The pressure of ice could have distorted the proportions and damage have occurred long ago.

He was not surprised when Izane said, "The mass is homogeneous and the metallic content is far too low for it to be a mechanical fabrication. There are traces of iron, but that is to be expected in this region. The mountains to the north are heavy with mineral deposits."

Veruchia was disappointed. "It couldn't be the ship?"

"I would stake my reputation that it is not. The material has all the attributes of solid rock." Izane made another adjustment. "Lower, Jarg. Lower. Right!" He gestured at the screen. "This is the highest definition possible with this apparatus. You can see the surface structure and the sonic probe reveals that the consistency is exactly the same as other rocks found in this area. I'm sorry, but this cannot possibly be anything else than a large deposit of natural stone."

Another failure. How many would there have to be before she gave up the search? She wouldn't give up; watching her face Dumarest knew that. She would go on looking until there was no time left. He smiled as Jarg sent the raft gliding towards the other selected point.

"Never mind. You didn't expect it to be easy."

"I was wrong," she said. "This area is not where the

ship is to be found. We'll check the other point to make sure, but I expect nothing." She frowned, thoughtful. "Earl, does a cyber lie?"

"They don't always tell the entire truth."

"Could they ever be wrong?"

"They could be. The accuracy of their predictions depends on the availability of data. Even a cyber needs facts to work on. You're thinking of what he told you about the Elgish Sea?"

"Yes, the area with the lowest order of probability. Earl, I wonder if he said that just to make me look elsewhere?"

"How long ago was it you asked?"

"A couple of years. No," she decided. "He couldn't have lied. There would have been no point in it. He couldn't possibly have known that I would ever seriously need to find the First Ship."

"You're wrong," said Dumarest. "Never underrate the Cyclan, and always remember that a cyber doesn't think like a normal person. To them everything is a matter of varying probability. *Everything.* He would have assessed your value and extrapolated a series of sequences of probable events stemming from a range of varying circumstances. It was inevitable that Chrozel would die. The only random factor was the time of his death, and even that could have been determined by appropriate action. At his death you stood in line to inherit. That was of such a low order of probability that it could almost have been ignored. If it had been higher you would be dead now."

"Assassinated?" Her face tensed. "Earl, are you serious? The cyber wouldn't do that."

"He wouldn't have to. A hint in the right ear and the

thing would have been done. Montarg is ambitious and would do anything to gain the Ownership. Of course Surat considered the possibility that you might press your claim. Naturally he took into account the chance that you might need to search for the proof which could lie in the First Ship. The probability would be so low as to be negligable but still it would be there. And if the Cyclan wanted Montarg to rule then he would have misguided you."

"He lied to me?"

"He didn't have to lie. He merely took two regions and told you that it was less likely the ship would be found in one than the other. Wend is a barren desert. Isn't it more probable that a thing could be found on land rather than in sea?"

The raft came to a halt. Izane worked his apparatus but Dumarest was sure what he would find. Another mass of rock or a compressed mound of frozen trees. Yet it was wise to be sure.

He moved away as Veruchia talked with the technician, standing close to the canopy as he looked at the stars. So many stars, lying in a thick band across the sky, some forming vague patterns; countless numbers of them, most with habitable worlds. For him some held memories; Derai with the hair like silver, Kalin with the hair like flame, Lallia and the strange woman he had met on Technos—steps on a journey it seemed would never end.

Which of those blazing suns shone on Earth?"

Montarg said, "Now!" and watched avidly as boys ran at each other with swords and shields. The swords were of wood, the shields of wicker; no great damage could be done, but they would learn. They would learn.

"A noble spectacle." Selkas was ironic. "Is that why you asked me here, Montarg? To watch youths revert to the beast?"

"They are in training." Montarg kept his eyes on the struggling boys. "And they are learning to shed an imposed artificiality. It is in the nature of man to fight. For too long we have denied that. What you see, Selkas, is the birth of a new culture."

"The resurrection of one long buried, Montarg. Teach violence to the subtenants and landless ones and where will it end? Dradea is a civilized world and I, for one, would like to see it remain so."

"Civilization is a relative term, Selkas. "I choose to call it decadence. Those boys will grow into men who do not shudder at the thought of violence. They will be accustomed to it, the better for having experienced the mystique of combat."

"Thugs, bravos, swaggerers who will regard all that is gentle as weakness. I have seen it on many worlds, Montarg. There are places where a person dare not walk undefended at night. You should visit them."

"I've no need to travel: Dradea is good enough for me."

"For you, perhaps." Selkas looked at the struggling boys. Several had fallen, some nursed bruises, many were crying with pain. "But what of those lads? What of the ones who desire to learn? We have only one biological laboratory on this planet, only one physics institute, only one small department of pure science. Compared to other worlds we are a village locked in ignorance. And you are encouraging that ignorance. Already ships are few and commerce low. Another generation and we shall be a forgotten world ignored by the rest of the galaxy."

"Perhaps," Montarg shrugged. "But better to own a viable world than one which has lost its pride. I would rather rule a dozen men than a million sheep."

"A laudable ambition—if true."

"You think I lie?"

"I think that you are a man obsessed," said Selkas deliberately. "A fanatic blinded by a misguided dream. This nonsense of the mystique of combat is not new. I have heard it before on other worlds and I have seen the inevitable result of those who have followed it. Men strutting like cockerels, armed, ready to kill at a word. Rigid formality and a stultyfing of the intellect. Such cultures cannot breed scientists and have no resources to spare for education. When every rich man needs to surround himself with retainers what chance is there for his money to build schools?"

"We could have both."

"Not with the state of our economy. Progress depends on a constantly expanding availability of funds which can be used for the development of art and science. Unless we have that surplus of wealth we can only regress. If you really want to help this world, close the arena and use the money to import teachers. A child can be taught at the cost of breeding a crell. A crell can only die—a child can grow to add to the wealth of this planet. Logic, Montarg. At times it is inescapable."

"Your logic, Selkas, not mine. But I did not invite you to join me to talk about that. I learn that Veruchia is now busy exploring the Elgish Sea."

"That is correct."

"Three hundred miles north at the village of Zem."

"Yes."

"Her and that scum from the arena." Montarg sneered. "Odd what steps some women will take to gratify their lust. It refutes your argument, Selkas. Veruchia, surely, is a cultured woman. She hates the games and all forms of violence and yet, despite that, she threw herself into the arms of a fighter, a transient who is snatching what he can get. When her money goes then so will he."

On the field, attendants moved among the injured, while others picked up the discarded swords and shields. One boy with a broken arm waited as they carried him away. Another had lost an eye, his face a mask of blood as he stumbled over the ground.

"They will know better the next time," said Montarg casually. He returned to the attack. "But don't worry, Selkas. Dumarest will not be able to gloat at having duped a foolish woman. I shall take care of that. You will be indebted to me for having saved your honor."

"Mine?"

"You threw them together. You provided the fire at which my cousin was burned."

"A fire need not burn," said Selkas quietly. "It can warm. For a lonely person it can be a great comfort."

"You care for her. Now I am sure of it and I wonder why. You defend her and support her in her stupidity. Two rafts, trained personnel, supplies and equipment without regard as to cost. Why, Selkas? Never before have you shown concern about any living thing. I am curious as to the reason."

"It's your money, Montarg."

He saw the scowl, the sudden blaze of fury, and tensed as Montarg lifted his hand, the fingers reaching for his sleeve. Then he shrugged, a man content to bide his time.

"The money you helped her to win. Yes, I know that, Selkas, you advised her to make the wager. She would never have done it alone. But you betrayed yourself then as you have betrayed yourself since. What is Veruchia to you? How could a man of your attainments be attached to a sullen, mutated freak?"

"Montarg! You go too far!"

"Do I, Selkas?" He gave his dog-laugh, soundless, horrible. "The truth is plain for all to see. But, I wonder, what caused the mutation? Both Lisa and Oued were of clear strain and neither had traveled off Dradea to where radiating suns could have disturbed their chromosomes. But you, Selkas, you traveled much and far. And, if old gossip is true, you and Lisa were very close at one time. Perhaps more than close."

"You're vile, Montarg. Despicable. It requires no courage to slander the dead."

"No greater courage than it takes to seduce the wife of a friend." He stepped back as Selkas moved forward, his fingers jerking at his sleeve, rising to show the metallic gleam of a laser. "Come closer and there will be a most regrettable accident. I was showing you this little toy when, somehow, it discharged itself into your face. I shall be most sorry—but you will be dead." His voice rose a little. "I warn you, Selkas!"

The field was deserted. They stood alone well beyond earshot of the others, the groups of parents and staff who had watched the battle. His word would be accepted and who would dare to antagonize the potential Owner? Selkas drew a deep breath and forced himself to relax. Incredibly he managed to smile.

"You flatter me, Montarg. Lisa was a beautiful woman. Do you think that if she had granted me her favors I would have kept silent? And is it really wise to impunge the ancestry of the next Owner?"

"Veruchia?" Montarg showed his amusement. His teeth gleamed in the sunlight as he holstered his weapon. "You're an optimist, Selkas. She has ten days left of the hundred granted by the Council. A short time in which to search an ocean."

"She could still be lucky."

"She could, but I doubt it. Miracles do not happen to order. In ten days time I shall be the new Owner of Dradea."

The weather was oppressive, the sun scorching as it hung in the air, the air heavy and still. Below where he stood on the cliffs Dumarest could see the water spread below, dark blue and green patched with the brown of drifting weed. Boats made creamy wakes as they headed outwards, the sound of their engines high and spiteful, thinned by distance. Closer to the shore other boats, powered by arms and sail, looked like fragile toys. From them men dived into the sea after molluscs, weed and marine growths of value.

Raising his eyes he could see the pair of rafts moving slowly a hundred feet above the water, following a carefully determined search pattern. Veruchia was on one, safe enough with the technicians and, Dumarest was convinced, safe enough until she found the proof she needed. There was no point in assassinating her before then.

"They won't find anything." The man at his side was thick and toughened by the sun. "My boys have scouted every inch of that area for shellfish and if anything laid on the bottom they would have found it. Right, Larco?"

His partner nodded. "That's right, Shem. From here to the edge of the continental shelf. But would those snots from the institute listen? Not them. They wouldn't take my word it was raining if they stood in a downpour."

"How do you work?" asked Dumarest. "Naked or with apparatus?"

"It depends how deep. Close to shore we go down straight but further out we use artificial lungs." Shem pointed. "See? About two miles. That's my boat and it's working the Coolum Bed. About a hundred and twenty feet. You could go down raw but with lungs you can really search the area. Some good stuff down there but it takes time to collect." His arm swung towards the north. "You don't get too much up there. The bottom's rough and the shelf comes in close. Further north still we don't bother."

"Why not?"

"Too dangerous. There's some big things out there, decapods, jellyfish, eels as thick as your body with jaws that could bite a man in half."

"The decapods are the worst," said Larco. "I've seen them big enough to pull down a ship. A fifty-man galley with outriggers."

"Bigger," said Shem. "Remember after that big storm? One of them got washed ashore and it took a week to get rid of it. The flesh isn't good for eating," he explained. "We had to grind it up small and sell it as fertilizer. They grow big, all right." He squinted at Dumarest. "You figure to go searching up north?"

"Maybe. Would you help?"

"To go down to the bottom?" Shem pursed his lips. "I

don't know about that. Maybe, if the money was good, but only maybe. It's too chancey down there. Life's hard enough as it is without looking for trouble. We'd like to help, but you know how it is."

"Yes," said Dumarest. "I know."

A boat took him out to where one of the rafts drifted high. It lowered at his signal, Izane complaining as he climbed aboard.

"You're disturbing the pattern. If you'd have waited another two hours we would have finished searching this area."

"We haven't got two hours." Dumarest was curt. "As far as I can see you're wasting time."

"I know my job."

"Admitted, but the fishermen know this area. Why didn't you take their advice?"

"Earl." Veruchia had been standing beside the scanning apparatus. She came forward and rested her hand on his arm. "We haven't time for quarrels."

"We haven't time to follow the book, either." Dumarest stared at the technician. "The fishermen know the bottom here as well as they know their own faces. I suggest we accept their word that the ship isn't in this area."

"They can't be sure of that," said Izane. "They could see it and never recognize it for what it was. By this time it would have accumulated a thick growth of molluscs and weed. The shape would have become distorted, other things. Before we can eliminate this region we must check every inch."

He pulled a sheaf of papers from a drawer and ran his finger over a mass of lines.

"See? We are on the edge of a continental fault. We know this area is prone to earthquakes and tremors and we know that a few centuries ago the coastline altered. If the ship had been close to the edge of the sea at that time, and there had been an earthquake, it is highly probable that both the land and the ship would have become submerged. Of course we can't be certain exactly where this happened, but this area shows the most promise."

The cold logic of scientific detachment pitted against local knowledge and the workings of intuition. Izane could be right and most probably was, but there was no time to make certain. For days they had scanned the area and time was running out.

Dumarest said, "There is a region to the north which remains unexplored. I think we should check it out."

"Random searching?" Izane's shrug expressed his contempt at the unscientific approach. "I can't agree that it would be wise. We could try a thousand spots by guesswork and miss what we are looking for. In order to be certain we must be precise."

An ocean to search, following the thin trail of rumor, geological maps and unreliable history. A lifetime could be spent inching along the coast alone.

Dumarest turned to face the woman. "Veruchia?"

He had thrown her the necessity of making a decision and she hesitated, reluctant to take the gamble.

"I don't know, Earl. We could be missing the only chance we have. Couldn't we speed up the search, Izane?"

"We are going as fast as we can. Faster and we may as well not bother at all. I advise that we continue the present pattern. Of course I must do as you decide. You are paying for the service."

His tone was peevish with fatigue. They were all tired

and numbed with constant failure, brains slow to function, tempers on edge. A bell chimed on the apparatus. Jarg checked it and shook his head.

"A mass of rock, large but of natural origin."

Veruchia sighed and then, womanlike, appealed to her lover. "I don't know what is best to do, Earl. Can't you decide?"

Without hesitation he said, "We'll go both north and south and scan the regions to either side of the fishing grounds out to the limits of the continental shelf. I suppose there is no point in extending the search beyond that point?"

"Not with our present equipment," said Izane. "The fall is sharp and the bottom deep. There is too much distortion to gain a clear picture. If we had a submersible I would advise it, but without—" He broke off, seeing no need for further explanation. "We go north then?"

"Immediately. Send the other raft to the south and report anything of interest." Dumarest took Veruchia by the arm. "You are going ashore. There's nothing you can do here and there's no sense in knocking yourself out. Izane knows what has to be done."

"How can I rest, Earl?"

"You'll rest." Drugs would take care of that and give her a dreamless sleep. "Jarg, signal a boat."

Veruchia relaxed, finding comfort in the touch of his hand, his obvious concern. It was good to have someone so close, a man to worry about her and see that things were attended to. Now there was nothing she need do but wait, no action to be taken but to sleep and hope that, this time, they would find the ship.

They had to. There was so little time.

VI

As he ran over the beach, Dumarest felt the quake, a minor tremor but enough to cause Veruchia to stumble. She would have fallen had he not caught her arm.

"Earl!"

"It's nothing." Shem was casual as he came towards them. "Just a twitch, and we get them often." He looked at Dumarest. "About that gear you asked me to have ready. You want me to put it aboard?" He gestured towards a heap of equipment, the waiting raft.

"No, there isn't room." Dumarest looked towards the south. The air was heavy, carrying a metallic taste, the sea leaden. "The other raft will be here soon. When it arrives throw out all the personnel aside from the driver and load your gear. How many men did you get?"

"Only me and Larco."

"Is that all?"

"I told you, the boys don't like that part of the coast. Neither do we but you made a fair offer and we're willing to take a chance. We might be able to get the Ven brothers when they come in but I can't promise."

"Get them," said Dumarest. "Send them after us with

123

the biggest boat they can get and with all the salvage equipment you can find. And don't waste time about it."

"Earl." Veruchia gripped his arm. "We can't be sure. All this could be a waste."

"We can afford to waste money," he said. "But not time. Let's move!"

Izane rustled papers as the raft lifted and headed towards the north. His normal impassivity had dissolved in the excitement of discovery.

"There!" His finger tapped a mass of flecks on the paper. "It is the only thing in the region we examined which holds any promise. Notice the shape? The metallic reading is far too high for it to be natural and it is not homogenous."

"Are you certain?" Veruchia fought to maintain her composure. "Have you checked?"

"Three individual times." Izane sobered a little. "Of course it may not be what you are looking for, and I must be frank, the chances are against it. The object could be another vessel or a large surface craft wrecked during a storm. It could even be a land installation which became submerged through the action of a tidal wave. It could even be a submarine construct or an accumulation of discarded material. Metal drums containing unstable compounds," he explained. "As yet we cannot be certain."

Dumarest was curt. "You made no investigation?"

"No. The object lies well below the surface and we had no undersea gear with us. I marked the position and came in to report. Incidentally, I must congratulate you on your foresight. I didn't think you would have had men and equipment organized."

Too few men and too limited equipment, but it was all

that was locally available. Dumarest moved to the front of the raft and looked at the sky, the sea. He felt restless, his skin prickling with tension. The raft slowed as a yellow float came into sight and halted just above it. Izane's voice echoed above the hum of his apparatus.

"You see?" He gestured at the screen. A mass of flecks marred the surface, some moving, others fading only to regain prominence. "Background noise," said the technician. "Fish and particles of drifting weed." He made adjustments. "I've raised the level so as to eliminate minor objects. That solid mass there is the edge of the continental shelf, you see how sharply it falls away. That is a mass of jumbled boulders and those are smaller ones. Note the irregularity. But here we have something unusual." His finger traced a longitudinal shape. "There!"

Somehow it was wrong. Dumarest studied it, trying to fit it into a familiar context. The ships he knew were longer, slimmer, far more graceful than the thing lying beneath the waves. But it would have become crusted with marine growths, he realized, and who could tell how spaceships had envolved from a time long ago?

He heard the sharp intake of Veruchia's breath. "Earl! We've found it!"

"We've found something." His tone was deliberately flat; it would be cruel to lift her hopes too high. "As Izane said it could be anything. There's only one way to find out." He called to the driver. "Take us down low. Get as close to the water as you can."

Veruchia frowned as he stripped and threw open the canopy. "What are you going to do, Earl?"

"Go and see what we've found." He retrieved the knife from his boot and looked around. "I want something heavy. Something we can afford to lose." He picked up a box of provisions. "This will do."

The weight cradled in his left arm, the knife gripped in his right hand, he stood for a minute, breathing deeply, hyperoxygenating his blood. Then he jumped from the raft into the sea.

The water was warm as it closed over his head, rapidly chilling as he plummeted towards the bottom. To one side he saw the thin cable of the marker and he kicked himself towards it, staying close to the guideline as he dropped. A patch of weed caught his foot, streaming upwards as he kicked it free, and tiny fish darted wildly in all directions. Pressure built in his ears and he swallowed, moving so as to fall head first, eyes strained in the thickening gloom.

A shape loomed vague and forbidding, crusted, wreathed with weed. He kicked himself towards it, releasing a thin stream of bubbles in an effort to ease the pressure which seemed to clamp him like a vice. The provisions fell away as he gripped an obtrusion with his left hand and pulled himself close. The blood pounded in his ears and his eyes felt as if they were being pressed back into his skull. He moved the knife forward, driving the sharp point against the crusted growths, trying to find a crack or fissure. The steel slipped into an opening and he wrenched, throwing his weight against the tempered metal. For a moment it resisted, yielding suddenly as a patch of shell fell aside. He struck again and felt the jar as the blade hit a denser medium. Scraping at it he caught the rasp and gleam of metal.

Bubbles streamed from his mouth as he rose to the surface. He kicked desperately in order to increase his speed of ascent, feeling the growing pain in his chest, the near-uncontrollable urge to open his mouth and gasp at the nonexistent air. The thing lay too deep and he had stayed too long.

The water brightened, a shimmering roof appearing above, a roof which broke in a shower of glistening droplets as he broke the surface. He rolled on his back, gasping, barely conscious, unaware of the blood which streamed from nose and ears. A shadow blotted out the sun and hands gripped him, hauling him aboard the raft.

Veruchia's eyes were bright, her face anxious. "Earl! Earl, my darling! You were down so long. I thought you were dead!"

He turned to rest face downwards, his weight supported on hands and knees. Gradually, as he sucked air into his aching lungs, his strength returned.

"I'm all right. But we'll need help to get down there."

"Is it—"

"It's something, and I'm sure that it's a ship. It could be the First Ship, but it's crusted and we'll need men and gear to work on it." Dumarest rose to his feet. "We'll get at it as soon as the others arrive."

Shem said, "You were lucky. The bottom here is too deep for natural diving. One of the boys could have done it but he'd have been trained from a child. You're strong," he said. "Tough, but you've got to respect the sea. If you don't it will kill you for sure. Have you used diving gear before?"

"I have," said Veruchia. "I spent a lot of time underwater when I was at university. We had a class in marine biology."

"You won't be coming down," said Shem curtly. He looked at Dumarest. "Well?"

"Once."

"Good, then I don't have to tell you what to do. Don't hold your breath on the way up, don't surface directly from the bottom, take your time and don't panic." He glowered at the water. "I don't like this," he said. "It's a bad area. We've lost too many boys around here. Right, Larco?"

"Right." His partner tightened a strap. Like Shem and Dumarest he was wearing bulky coveralls grotesque with added padding. Tubes from air cylinders on his back ran to a mouthpiece. A goggle eyemask contained radiophonic equipment. Each man was armed with a heavy knife and a gun firing explosive darts.

Dumarest said, "What about the others? Are they coming?"

"The Ven brothers are on their way. It will be easier to work from a boat but I guess you don't want to wait for them. One other thing." Shem nodded at Izane's apparatus. "I guess that thing can tell if anything big moves through the water, right?"

"Yes," said Izane.

"Then if you see anything let us know at once. Don't wait to find out what it is and don't be curious. If you see something big moving our way give us the word."

The technician looked puzzled. "What do you expect?"

"The worst." Shem was grim. "There's some nasty creatures in the deeps and quakes tend to unsettle them. There've been a few twitches and they could be restless. Damn it," he exploded with sudden violence. "I must be crazy to do this!"

"You don't have to," said Veruchia. "I can take your place."

"That's what I'm afraid of. If I let a woman go down

128

because I was scared I'd never be able to look my wife in the face again. Well, let's get on with it."

It was different from the last time. Now he drifted down, weightless, almost floating, gliding through the water without effort. Dumarest could hear the rush of bubbles from his mouthpiece and see them rise from his companions, the goggles giving perfect visibility. Within minutes they were on the bottom. He heard a voice in his ear.

"Hell, look at that! The damn thing's poised on the edge."

Shem's voice was distorted by his throat-mike. Larco answered.

"It's ready to fall. One good twitch and it'll be over. It's a long drop if it does."

Dumarest kicked himself upwards and circled the area. The vessel hung poised on the edge of an undersea cliff, part of its mass suspended over the rim. They were at the limit of the continental shelf.

He glided over an unknown depth of water as a bird would circle the edge of a precipice, kicking his legs so as to come close to the massive bulk. An opening gaped along one side: the open port of the cargo hold, he guessed. It was easy to guess what must have happened.

The ship would have been on apparently firm ground. There had been an earthquake; the sea had withdrawn to return in an overwhelming flood. Water had gushed into the vessel and it had been carried back into the sea by the retreating tidal wave. It would have rolled for miles before coming to rest. A little further and it would have been lost forever.

"All right, Earl," said Shem. "You're the boss. Where do we start?"

129

If the ship still contained anything of value it would be in the control room. Dumarest kicked himself forward to join the others and stood looking at the crusted shape. The cargo holds were always towards the base of every ship he had known and it was logical to assume this one would follow the pattern. The control room would be towards the nose. He measured the proportions, baffled by the odd dimensions. Here? A little further back? More forward? There would be an emergency airlock which would give direct access if he could find it.

"We've got to strip the crust," he said. "Start from about five yards back from the end. How will you do it?"

"Smash it loose with hammers." Shem stooped over the heap of tools dropped down from the raft. "We should have powered equipment," he grumbled. "Heavy-duty lasers. It'll take a long time using muscle."

Selkas was bringing more equipment from the city, but until he arrived muscles were all they had. Dumarest picked up a heavy hammer and swung it at the encrustation. The thing moved slowly, hampered by the water, the head landing with deceptive force. He swung again, then a third time and calcareous matter crumpled.

Shem grunted. "It could be a lot worse. In more shallow water it would be yards thick. This shouldn't take too long." He picked up a hammer. "Keep a sharp watch, Larco."

Larco patted his gun. "I'm watching, Shem."

Dumarest's arms began to ache. It took tremendous effort to swing the heavy hammer through the crushing water and the coveralls and padding hampered every movement. He was relieved by Larco, relieving Shem in turn, chafing at their slow progress. The deposit had to be pounded loose and scraped free but eventually a cleared section of metal was exposed to the light.

"Ten minutes and we head upwards," said Shem. "The tanks are getting low."

"Just a minute." Dumarest was studying the cleared area. Fragments of paint clung to the surface and he tried to fit them into a recognizable pattern. Identifying marks? A guide for external forces to reach the emergency port in case of need? He cleared away more of the deposit and saw the rim of a port.

"Come on, Earl." Larco drifted beside him. "It's a ship right enough," he mused. "Maybe we should try getting in from the inside. The hold's open, if it is a hold, and maybe—" He broke off as the ground heaved beneath their feet. "A quake!"

It came again, and then a third time far more intense than before. Dumarest felt himself gripped by invisible forces and thrown high to one side, spinning, buffeted by shifting masses of water. The ship lifted, slowly, seemed to hesitate for a long moment and then fell back on the ledge. It slipped a little towards the edge of the chasm and then came to rest.

From the depths something rose like a plume of smoke.

It was an eel, attracted by the hammering, frightened by the sudden quake. The sinuous body was thirty feet long and spined like the edge of a saw. The barrel-sized head was crested, the gaping jaws lined with rows of gleaming teeth. It poised, watching the three men. Larco was the closest.

"Shem! For God's sake!"

A streak of fire spat towards the creature and missed, the dart exploding against the hull of the ship. Again Shem fired, this time managing to hit the end of the long body. It did nothing to slow the beast down. Like an arrow it sliced through the water, intent on its prey.

"Shem!"

Larco screamed as the jaws closed on his body, the teeth shearing through the padding and coverall. Blood rose like a mist.

Dumarest twisted, fighting to gain control of his movements. He kicked himself towards the giant eel and raised the squat barrel of his gun. Sighting was difficult and the weapon strange. His first shot missed; the second tore a great hole in the flesh a third of the way from the head. The next followed it and almost cut the creature in half.

Larco screamed again. "Shem!"

Shem was aiming for the head. He swam close, his gun extended in both hands, his finger clamped on the trigger to empty the magazine in a burst of continuous fire. The screaming died as head and man dissolved into pulp.

"Up!" His voice was harsh over the radio. "Up before the blood attracts more of the things." He was choking as they neared the surface. "Larco. Dear God, how shall I tell his wife?"

Izane lifted his hands in a protective gesture. "I didn't know. You've got to believe that. The quake disturbed my instruments. I didn't see anything to warn you about."

"You bastard!" Shem stepped forward, his face ugly. "I've a mind to smash your face in. I told you to watch. I relied on you, we all did, and you let us down. Larco's dead. I killed him, you understand? I had to kill him. A friend and my partner and I had to kill him."

Dumarest said, "You had no choice."

132

"You think it was easy?"

"I know it wasn't, but if you hadn't done it I would have."

"You should have," said Shem. He looked suddenly old. "Then I wouldn't have had to live with it. You could have saved me from that."

"And left you wondering if you lacked the guts?"

Veruchia looked from one to the other, not understanding but aware they lived in a different world than the one she knew: men of action, facing danger, each relying on the other for help if it could be given, merciful death if it could not. And it had been Shem's right and duty to make the decision.

She wondered if she could kill Dumarest if the need ever arose. She had no doubt that he could kill her.

Such thoughts were depressing, casting a shadow over their success, adding to that already thrown by Larco's death. She moved to Izane's side and looked at the screen of his machine. It was alive with movement. Even as she watched a blotched shape came moving in from the deeps, a gross body wreathed with many arms. Narrow lines darted from its approach.

She called to Shem. "Something's happening. Could you explain?"

He grunted as he joined her. "A decapod and more of those damned eels. Trust the scent of blood to bring them on the run. I told you this part of the coast was dangerous."

"But they won't stay there, will they?"

"No," said Dumarest. "They'll leave when they find no food." He could sense and understand her anxiety. Now they had found the ship further delay was intolerable, but it could not be helped. To reassure her he said,

"We've found the airlock. Once the area is clear we'll go down and burn it open."

"We?" Shem scowled and shook his head. "Not me and I doubt if you'll find anyone else. If you want to go down there you'll have to go alone. I'm not following Larco."

"Izane?"

The technician frowned. "My men are not used to undersea work. And, to be frank, they would not be willing after what has happened. We could hire experienced divers, of course, but I doubt if we have the time."

"We have time," said Veruchia. "There are still a few days left."

"I wasn't talking of the contractual time," said Izane. "We are in an unstable region and on the edge of an intercontinental fault. There have been several minor tremors in the past few hours and there will be more. At least one far more severe. The ship is poised on the edge of an undersea cliff. Any serious disturbance will cause it to lose equilibrium and, if it does, it will fall into the chasm. I predict that such a shock will occur within a matter of hours."

Dumarest took a deep breath, remembering how the ship had lifted, settled and slipped towards the edge. "Can you be certain?"

"That the ship will fall? From what you have told me, yes."

"That there will be a major shock within a few hours."

"I am a geologist and have studied volcanic activity and earthquakes. The pattern is a classic one for regions like this. The only doubt is as to the exact time."

Another gamble. Dumarest weighed the odds as he looked at the screen. The Ven brothers had a laser and they would arrive shortly. It wouldn't take long to burn open the outer door, then a little more time to get inside and search the control room. They could carry lights if it were dark, so nightfall would be no problem. But lights could attract the beasts from the deeps. If they did they could be used as a defensive weapon; eyes accustomed to darkness would be vulnerable to a brilliant shaft of light. And there were other measures which could be taken.

"Get back to the village," he told Shem. "I want all the nets you can lay your hands on. The strongest you can find. Cable too. And floats. We'll rig a screen around the ship."

"It won't work." The fisherman was emphatic. "You saw that eel. We haven't a net in the village that would hold it. And you'd still need me to set them in position. I'm sorry, Earl, but it can't be done. Given time and the right materials, maybe, but not as things are."

Nets were out then. Dumarest looked thoughtfully at the screen. "You say blood attracts those creatures. How about taking the raft and moving out a little way? Catch a fish and use it for bait. Spill the blood of whatever comes after it. Could you do that?"

"Sure. That's how we catch the decapods. Not that we ever want to, but sometimes a few rich people fancy going on a hunt. When they do we set a ring of boats, lay some bait and they sit high and safe in a raft to shoot it down. Once we actually caught one for the Institute. Stunned it with sonic shock. God knows what they did with it or why they wanted it alive."

"For export," said Veruchia. "I remember the incident. A museum ship arrived and wanted a specimen for Carne. That was years ago."

"That's what we'll do," Dumarest decided. "We'll go back to the village, get men and boats and return. We can tow the boats so as to save time. When you're all set I'll go down to the ship."

"Alone?" Shem snorted. "That's a sure way to commit suicide. How are you going to keep watch while you're working?"

"I'll go down with him," said Veruchia.

Shem stared at her. "You'll do what? After what happened to Larco? Are you raving mad?"

"I've no choice," she said flatly. "I can't expect you to understand but I've got to get into that ship. If this is the only chance I have then I must take it. You'll hire me your gear?"

"No."

"The Ven brothers will have some. I'll use theirs."

She met his eyes, sensing his indecision, knowing better than to offer him more money. If he agreed to help it would be because she was a woman and desperate and needing his skill and strength. His pride would not permit him to remain on the surface while she went below. And she was going, he knew it.

His shrug was surrender. "All right, I'll help you. But just one thing. If anything happens to me be sure and take care of my family."

The night had brought eeriness, turning the bottom into a place of brooding mystery speared by the brilliance of their lights. Colors followed the beams, bright reds and yellows, unsuspected greens and aching blues. Fronds of weed drifted like menacing ghosts and tiny fish gleamed like living jewels as they moved towards the ship.

A jellyfish drifted close, tendrils set to sting. It died beneath Shem's crushing hand.

"Damn things," he muttered. "Is everything all right up there?"

Izane's voice replied. "No movement in your vicinity of any kind. The second raft reports intense activity in the region of the assembled boats."

That was miles away where the Ven brothers had spilled barrels of bait and the carcasses of slaughtered beasts. So far everything was going according to plan.

Dumarest reached the cleared portion of the ship. Veruchia, bulky in her protective clothing drifted at his side. "The lock, Earl?"

"I think so. In fact I'm sure of it." He had picked up one of the discarded hammers. "I'm going to knock the rest of this stuff off the panel. Stand watch while I do it and Veruchia, be careful."

She set down the laser and hefted her gun. A flashlight had been set along the barrel. A second light was strapped to her head and a third hung at her belt. "I'll be careful."

She moved aside as he set to work, standing with the vessel at her back, head moving as she scanned the area. Shem stood at Dumarest's far side. He was uneasy, regretting his decision, weakened by his knowledge of the threatening sea. If an eel should come darting from the gloom there would be little time to spot it before it attacked—no time at all to escape. It would be a matter of centering in the beam of the torch mounted on the gun, blinding it, and shooting it to death before it could recover. And a decapod would be worse: slower, but harder to kill and slower to die.

He shuddered at the thought of arms closing around him, crushing him to death.

What had Larco thought when the jaws had gripped him? A moment of unbelief, perhaps, until the teeth had started to bite and the blood to flow, and then there could only have been horror, the terrible realization that he was going to die and that nothing could save him. Had he welcomed the darts which had ripped him apart?

Shem moved uneasily, not liking such thoughts and knowing they were dangerous. This was no time for brooding. A moment's inattention and he could follow his late partner. Would Marth grieve for long?

He heard the rasp of Dumarest's breath and said, "Best take a break now, Earl. I'll take over."

It was good to lose his anxiety in work. He slammed the hammer against the hull, knocking away sheets of encrustation. The deposit came away easier now; the jar the ship had received must have loosened the coating and soon the entire port was clear. He hit it a few times to knock away the crusting over the handle and hinges. Maybe they wouldn't have to use the laser.

Izane's voice whispered in his ear: "Something long and narrow approaching from the depths."

Another eel! Shem dropped the hammer and snatched up his gun, the beam of light flashing from side to side as he traversed the weapon. Beneath the goggles sweat stung his eyes.

Dumarest said, "Veruchia, stand beneath the port with your back to the ship, have your gun ready and look towards the shore. Shem, you stand to her right and look beyond her to your left. I'll take the other side." And then, to Izane: "How close and from which direction?"

"About three hundred yards and to the southwest. It's moving very slowly."

"The lights have made it curious," said Shem. "That and the hammering." He swung his gun in a wide circle, its beam joining that from his helmet. "We've got a blind spot. It could come up behind the ship and be on us before we know it. We should have had another man at least."

Another dozen would have been better, but he had been the only fool in the village. He squinted at the air-gauge, a reflex action quickly learned by all divers, but there was no need for concern. They carried extra tanks and had plenty of air. Guiltily he returned to his vigil: that moment of inattention could have cost a life.

Dumarest said, "Izane?"

"It's still drifting, no, it's turning in a circle and heading towards the depths."

Veruchia relaxed, conscious of the strain, the tension of bone and muscle. She had stood concentrating on the area before her, afraid even to blink. "It's gone, Earl."

"It could come back," said Shem. "Those things are fast." He hesitated, wanting to suggest they return to the surface but knowing the woman would never agree. And, if she stayed, so would Dumarest, and how could he desert them now? He compromised. "Let's give it a little longer. It could come back with others."

They waited five minutes and then got back to work. Dumarest ran his fingers around the edge of the port, eyes close to the surface, the beam of his helmet light reflected in a glowing halo so that he seemed to be limned with radiance.

"We may not have to burn it open," he said. "It would save time if we didn't." More important a sudden rise in local temperature could attract unwanted visitors. "Izane?"

"Nothing is moving in your immediate vicinity." The technician sounded worried. "But there has been another tremor to the south. A minor one, the shockwave dampened before it could reach you. I suggest that you waste no time."

Dumarest gripped the handle of the port, pulled and felt the grate of metal. He rested both feet to either side and used the full force of back and shoulders as he pulled again. The handle rose. He jerked at it but lacked traction, his pull causing him to glide forward over the lock.

"Use a hammer," advised Shem as he regained his position. "Here, let me." He swung the massive tool against the edge of the uplifted metal. Again, a third time. At the next blow the handle yielded, swinging down to the open position. "Right," he said. "That's freed the catch. Now let's see if we can get it open."

Among the tools was a crowbar, three inches thick, twelve feet long, curved so as to give maximum leverage, one end flattened. Shem grunted as he rammed the thin edge under the rim of the port.

"Help me, Earl. Use the hammer to drive it in. Once we get a grip we can lever it up." He swore as the panel resisted. "Damn it, what's holding it now?"

Veruchia said, "It must still be watertight. The interior's full of air. We'll have to burn a hole and equalize the pressure. Earl?"

"A minute. Izane?"

"Still clear. Two narrow shapes about a quarter of a mile towards the depths. One closer but very deep."

The laser was designed for surface use, inefficient

below the waves. It would work but it would take time to burn a hole. And the water would absorb the heat and diffuse it. Dumarest studied the port. The weight of water pressing against the panel would hold it shut but the merest crack would allow the escape of the air inside, the entry of water to equalize the pressure. He gripped the bar and swung his feet so they rested on the hull.

"Join me, Shem. Together now." They heaved, muscles cracking beneath the strain. "Veruchia."

She added her strength, straightening her legs so as to gain the advantage of the long muscles of thighs and calves, the bar across her shoulders, back and loins adding extra pressure. A long moment broken only by the rasp of labored breathing and then she felt a slight movement, another . . . then a gush of bubbles rose from the edge of the port.

"Once more."

This time it was easier. A moment of strain and then the water boiled with a great stream of released air. She drifted to the bottom as the two men swung wide the port. It moved easily; ancient science had known the use of noncorrosive alloys and inherent lubrication.

"Earl!" Excitement made her voice shrill. "The inner port's intact. I could close the outer one and go inside. Think what this means, Earl! Everything inside is just as it was. Nothing could have been spoiled by the water. Earl!"

Success was intoxicating. She dived towards the open port intent on getting the proof she needed, for which she had searched so long. Izane's voice was an irritating buzz.

"Danger! Two shapes approaching fast from the

141

depths!" His voice rose a little. "They are now very close!"

"Watch it, Earl!" Shem crouched on the bottom, beams of light swinging from helmet and gun. He swore as a glistening shape lanced like a living jewel above and to one side, his darts vanishing harmlessly into the murk. "Damn it! We haven't a chance!"

A second eel joined the first, attracted by the disturbance of the escaping air, cautious of the lights. There was no time to take up their previous positions. Veruchia was at the mouth of the port, almost inside the lock itself, and Dumarest flicked at the panel, closing it behind her. At least she would be safe beneath the protection of the thick metal.

"Earl?"

"Stay where you are." Dumarest threw himself towards Shem where he crouched on the bottom. Their only hope of survival was to work in harmony, each covering the other. "Watch my back," he snapped. "I'll do the same for you. Wait until they attack then fire. Don't waste darts on bad targets."

"The woman?"

"She's safe." Dumarest tensed as an eel lunged towards them. He raised his gun, finger on the trigger, forcing himself not to fire. The distance was too great and the chance of missing too high. As he watched the eel twisted away from his lights, the sheen of its body a ribbon of silver.

Izane's voice echoed in his ear: "Another two shapes moving from the west. A third rising from the depths."

"Earl!"

"Quiet and concentrate!" There was no time for conversation, no concentration to spare. They had to sit and wait for the eels to attack, for the great heads to come directly towards them, jaws wide, eyes gleaming, then and only then to fire, sending the explosive darts down the gullet, through the roof of the mouth and into the brain.

"To the left, Earl. The left!"

Shem's left. Dumarest twisted to his right and saw the monster in his lights. A second shape came from one side in a concerted attack, both coming from towards the land.

"Take the one to your left," snapped Dumarest. "And wait."

Wait until they were too close to miss, until the heads grew huge in the cold beam of the lights and they could feel the pressure of the water sent ahead. Shem fired, his darts lancing high, lowering as he depressed the barrel of his gun. Dumarest followed, clamping his finger tight, seeing the darts hit the sloping upper jaw and vanish between the teeth. Blood, skin and shattered bone flowered in the lights and rushed towards them. The eels were dead but still had their original momentum, dying reflex adding to their speed.

Dumarest felt the surge of water as they passed over him, the lash of the current as it threw him to one side. Shem cried out, incoherently, his lights pinwheeling in the darkness.

Both bodies slammed against the vessel at the same time.

"Earl! What has happened?"

"Veruchia!" Dumarest turned so as to throw his lights on the vessel. "For God's sake, girl! Get out of there!"

The ship was moving. The slamming impact of both dead eels had disturbed its balance, massed tons tipping the scale. As Dumarest watched it rolled a little and then, with deceptive slowness, began to slip over the edge.

"Veruchia!"

He dived towards it, feeling the encrustation beneath his fingers, pulling himself towards the port. Shem's voice screamed in his ears.

"For God's sake, Earl, let's get out of here! More eels are coming!"

Dumarest ignored the warning, kicking himself towards the port, fighting his own bouyancy as the ship gathered speed. It was a losing battle. He felt the scrap of metal as he caught the rim and then the ship had vanished, falling from beneath him as its inert mass carried it like a stone to the bottom far below.

VII

It was early dawn, the canopy pearled with light, the bowl of the sky tufted with fleecy cloud. Dumarest lay watching them. He felt oddly detached as he had once felt in an arena when his foot had slipped and he had fallen waiting for death. That had been many years ago now, too many for him to remember the name of the world. A friend had saved him then as a friend had saved him now. He moved and felt the ache of his lungs, recognizing the taste of blood in his mouth.

Selkas moved towards him as he sat upright. He looked older than Dumarest remembered, lines dragging from nose to mouth, shadows deepening his eyes. Even his voice had lost its undertone of cynical amusement.

"How do you feel?"

"Not good." Dumarest looked at his naked body. One leg was torn, the wound clear beneath a transparent coating. "When did you arrive?"

"While you were below. I saw them pull you from the water."

"And Shem?"

"You were the only one."

147

Dumarest had known it, memory was all too clear: the frantic need to escape and reach the safety of the rafts before the other predators should arrive, more drawn by the scent of blood. They hadn't made it. Shem had fired all his darts too soon. His screams had been mercifully brief.

Another gamble, thought Dumarest bleakly. Life was full of them. Two men in the sea and one had to die. Even odds and again he had won. Shem had lost and Veruchia.

"She should never have gone below," he said. "I should never have permitted it."

"Could you have stopped her?"

"Yes."

"By force, you would have had to use that. Izane has told me of the need for haste. The shock he predicted came minutes after you surfaced. Nothing could have prevented the ship from falling over the edge."

"She gambled for the ownership of a world," said Dumarest. "And she lost. A little time, she said, a hundred days and some money. She never thought to risk her life."

"She isn't dead, Earl." Selkas looked like a ghost in the pearly light. "She radioed on the way down. She managed to open the inner port and the control room was intact. After all these years under the sea it was still watertight. They built well in the old days." His tone became bitter. "Perhaps too well. It would have been better, perhaps, for the plating to have collapsed beneath the pressure. It didn't. And now she's down there, locked in an ancient tomb. Waiting to die."

Waiting? Dumarest frowned. Even if the air in the compartment had been breathable it couldn't have lasted long, not even with the air she had carried in the tanks. Already the carbon dioxide content must be at a level dangerously high. Then he remembered that the air would have lasted longer than he was calculating. She would be under normal pressure, not crushed beneath tons of water with the need to compensate.

"No." Selkas had read his thoughts or followed the inevitable train of reasoning. "We can't save her. Izane?"

"The ship is far too deep." Like Selkas the technician showed his fatigue. "There is a limit to what unprotected flesh can stand and the vessel is far beyond it. With appropriate armor a man might just stand a chance but he would be weighed down, helpless, and what could he do? Once the hull is opened the girl will be crushed to death. It might be possible to attach buoyancy devices to lift the vessel but, again, that would take many men and we have no armor or equipment. Getting them would take too much time; even in her present condition she would be dead long before we could begin."

Dumarest looked at Selkas. "What does he mean?

"She has taken quick-time, Earl. She found some vials of drugs, old but she thought still fit for use. She knew the air could not last and she hoped—" He broke off, biting his lips. "There is no hope. She has merely delayed the inevitable and extended her agony."

Extended it by a factor of forty-to-one. Even if the air would normally last only a few hours she had stretched it to more than a week. Yet still there wasn't enough time. It would take longer than that to construct armor, arrange for large surface vessels, find men and begin the salvage. And the predators lurking in the deeps would still make rescue impossible.

But she was alive and waiting, hoping, perhaps, for a

miracle. Dumarest looked at his hands, thinking of others skeined with black, of a face similarly marked, of the lovely lines of a body beautiful in its natural adornment —thinking too of the child within the woman. She had given him her trust and he had failed her. If he hadn't shut her in the airlock . . . if he had taken a little more care in killing the eels . . . if he had insisted that she stay on the surface . . .

"Earl." Selkas gripped his arm. "Stop tormenting yourself, man. It wasn't your fault."

Dumarest shrugged off the hand. "Get me the Ven brothers. Hurry!"

"What—"

"Get them!"

He dressed and stood looking down at the assembled boats—the fast raft Selkas had ridden, the others loaded with equipment they could not use. The rising sun gilded them with touches of red and gold, the sea with green and amber. Against the water the sound of voices was thin and distant.

To the hard-faced men who later boarded the raft he said, "I want you to catch a decapod for me. A big one. Can you do it?"

One of the twins said, "Sure. But we'll need some equipment and it won't be cheap."

"I want it alive. Stunned."

"That won't be easy," said the other. "Those things are hard to handle."

Dumarest was curt. "You've done it before. If you haven't, find those who have. Izane will help you to track one down and you can use our equipment. And you'll be well paid. I want one caught, stunned and waiting by the time I get back." To Selkas he said, "now take me to the city. Fast!"

The director of the Dradean biological laboratory said, "I understand from Selkas that you have a problem you wish to discuss. I trust that it is important; there are experiments which need my attention."

He was old, like his desk, the chairs, the curtains at the window. The building itself showed signs of neglect and Dumarest could guess the rest: an institution lacking financial support; a home of science out of favor with those in power at present—or those who had been in power. The late Owner had left his mark. The equipment would be old, the personnel few, materials scarce. But it was all that was available.

Dumarest said, "I need your help, director. You are the only man on Dradea who can give it to me. I understand that you are familiar with the life sciences and I want you to give me the use of your facilities, your training and your skill."

Amplon frowned, uneasy at the unusual request. He had anticipated a demand for a subtle drug with which to capture the favor of a woman or something to give amorous strength to a male. Such requests were common, so low had the laboratory fallen.

"You can help me? You do have the skill?"

Amplon said, dryly, "As a young man I studied on Atin and later on Orge. I was the head of my class and was permitted to instigate my own projects. Yes, I think you can say that I have a little skill in my profession."

"I was referring to the technicians available."

"I have a very clever young man. In fact he is brilliant. If things were different he would now be a director of his own institution. However, that is beside the point. Just how can I help you?"

Dumarest reached for paper and pencil and drew fifteen symbols in random order. "Are these familiar to you?"

Amplon studied them. "They appertain to the life sciences?"

"Yes."

"Then they are the symbols for molecular units. I am familiar with the coding. The construction of such units is a normal part of any biological laboratory." He looked curiously at Dumarest. "How is it that you are conversant with the life sciences?"

Dumarest ignored the question. "Are you equipped to manufacture these units?"

"Yes, but—"

"Then please do so and please do it as fast as you possibly can."

"You didn't let me finish," said Amplon. His dignity was offended. "This isn't a shop or factory where you can demand instant service. The equipment necessary for the construction of these units is at present engaged on a series of experiments. It will require time to complete them and more time to do as you request." The director paused, then added, "That is, if I agree to cooperate at all. As yet you have given me no reason why I should."

Time! Dumarest looked at the window, bright with sunlight. It had taken hours to get to the city from where the ship had fallen and it would take as long to get back. More time to construct the units and even more to assemble them. How to convince the director of the need for haste? The truth? He could have no love for the present situation and must know what to expect if Montarg should inherit. The truth, then, but not all of it.

Amplon looked puzzled as Dumarest told him the facts.

"But I can't see how these units could possibly help."

"Isolated, no, but formed into a chain they might." Dumarest forestalled the obvious question. "I am not going to tell you how and I am not going to tell you the order in which they must be assembled. All I want you to do is to construct them. I shall assemble them myself."

"You have the skill?"

Dumarest remembered the long hours he had spent learning the necessary manual dexterity, the longer months spent at a handful of laboratories where the resident technicians had considered him a dabbling amateur.

"Yes," he said. "I have the skill."

"Redal will help you if you need assistance. He is the young man I spoke about. I shall put him in charge of the project."

"And you will start at once? Selkas will meet all expense," urged Dumarest. "Perhaps that isn't important to you; if not, remember this. Once Montarg inherits, your skills will be devoted to the breeding of beasts for the arena. This building could become a training school for fighters. If you and your profession hope to survive on Dradea then you dare not waste a second."

Once decided, Amplon was a man of action. "I shall commence at once. Give me twelve hours and—"

"Twelve?"

"It will take that to construct the units. They need time to grow and formulate their characteristics and they must be checked to determine whether or not they have developed undesirable traits." Amplon rose from behind his desk. "Even with speeded techniques it cannot possibly be done in less. Twelve hours."

Dumarest glanced through the window at the sun. It was almost noon. Allowing time for the assembly and the return, it would be as late before he could be back where the ship rested on the bottom of the Elgish Sea. If the Ven brothers did their job it would leave less than a day before the hundred allowed by the Council had expired.

Time enough if Veruchia remained alive. If she had found the proof she needed. If nothing went wrong.

Selkas was waiting outside. He fell into step as Dumarest strode down the shabby corridor, the sunlight harsh on his face as they stepped outside. A bench stood beside a small pool in which floated waxen flowers. A fish leapt from the surface as they sat, golden, dripping rubies.

"Earl?"

"If Amplon isn't a liar and if he does as he promised, Veruchia can be saved."

Selkas drew in his breath. He had followed Dumarest blindly, obeying his orders for want of a better course of action, but he could not understand what a biological laboratory had to do with salvaging a vessel lying on the bottom of an ocean.

He watched as another fish sprang from the water, vanishing in a glittering spray of droplets.

"Earl, I must know what you intend to do. I can't sit here, doing nothing, while Veruchia waits for death."

"There is nothing you can do, Selkas."

"Do you think I don't know that? For God's sake, Earl. If there is hope let me share it!"

Dumarest sensed his pain. Quietly he said, "You love her?"

"Not in the way you mean, but yes, I love her. To me she is the most important thing on this world. I would give all I possess to see her standing in the sun, alive and well, smiling, calling me by name." Selkas fought to regain his composure, conscious that the mask, had slipped, the armor behind which he faced life, had slipped. "Please, Earl. If there is a chance let me know."

Dumarest hesitated, weighing the need for secrecy against the other's need for reassurance. It would be too cruel to remain silent.

"There is a chance," he said abruptly. "On a world remote from Dradea I came into possession of a special technique devised in a hidden laboratory. It is the construction of an artificial symbiote named an affinity-twin. It consists of fifteen molecular units and the reversal of one makes it either dominant or subjective. Injected into the bloodstream it nestles in the base of the cortex, meshing with the thalamus and taking control of the entire nervous and sensory systems. In other words the being with the dominant half of the affinity-twin takes over the body of the host which has the subjective half. Need I tell you what that means?"

Complete domination; the intelligence of one man placed in the body of another—or the intelligence of a man being placed in the body of a beast. Selkas drew in his breath.

"The decapod?"

"Yes."

"But will it work?"

If it didn't Veruchia would die and Dumarest with her. He looked at his hands, the bare fingers of the left, thinking of the ring, the love-gift of Kalin. Kalin with the green eyes and flame-red hair. Brasque had given her the secret he had stolen from the Cyclan and died. She had given it to him and died—not the shell she had worn but the real woman whose personality had given it life. The ring had held the secret of the correct sequence in which the units should be assembled. The ring was gone now but the secret remained locked fast in his mind—

—The secret the Cyclan would give worlds to possess because, with it, they would own the galaxy: their puppets in every position of power; the mind of a cyber in every ruler and person of influence. No wonder they hunted him with growing desperation.

The driver said, "God, look at that thing! The size of it!" His voice was shrill with disbelief.

Below the sea was alive with boats of every size. To one side Dumarest could see the rafts moving slowly as they scanned the water. One changed course as they approached and headed towards them— Izane, probably, coming to make his latest report. Dumarest concentrated on the scene below.

The Ven brothers had done their job. In a wide circle of boats, lying flaccid on the surface, a bloated shape spread multiple arms in the afternoon sun.

It was huge, the body a hundred yards in length, the arms doubling the expanse, a tremendous mass of flesh and sinew a dull blue in the sunlight, the arms covered with suckers and wreathed with spines. As he watched the arms quivered, lifted a little, slamming down on the water and sending showers of spray high into the air. It fell quiescent as the sharp bark of sonic explosions rent the air.

Selkas said, "Earl, you can't. Not in that thing. It isn't possible."

"It has a brain and a bloodstream. It's possible." If he had assembled the units correctly. If they worked on creatures of differing species. If the hastily constructed units had formed true.

There had been no time for checks or testing. Dumarest closed his eyes, fighting the waves of fatigue dulling his brain. It had been a long night with him working with Redal and the director, urging them on, forcing the pace, making certain that no time was wasted. And then he had locked them out of the laboratory as, alone, he had put his learned skill to the test. Afterwards he had destroyed all trace of his activities. If he should die the secret of the correct sequence would die with him.

A jerk of the raft snapped him awake and fully aware.

Izane had come alongside and he had the Ven brothers with him. They scowled as Dumarest followed by Selkas jumped on the raft.

"How long do you want us to hold that thing?" one demanded. "We expected you before this."

"We were delayed. Is everything under control?"

"For the moment, yes." The other stared down at the stunned creature. "We lost two boats and three men getting that. And if you don't hurry there won't be anything left. Those damned eels will tear apart anything which can't protect itself. What the hell do you want it for anyway?"

"That's my business. Can you get any men who are willing to go under?"

"Divers?" One of the brothers stared his disbelief. "After what happened to Shem and Larco?"

"Try and find some. Report to Selkas if you do," Dumarest waited until they had left, dropping from the raft into a waiting boat. To Izane he said, "You have the ship spotted?"

"Three markers set as close as I can determine. It was impossible to be more precise, the ship is very deep."

"And Veruchia?"

"Nothing as yet."

It was an added complication. Dumarest drew Selkas to one side and said in a low voice, "Keep trying to contact her. With any luck at all the quick-time she took would have lost some of its potency and she could recover her normal metabolism at any time. Don't let her take more. If she gets in contact tell her to wear her breathing gear and to burn a hole in the outer lock when Izane gives the word. That will equalize the pressure and allow her to escape. I'll try to get the ship back on the continental shelf. If I can't I'll get it as near to the surface as I can. If she doesn't recover you'll have to get divers to go down after her. Offer them a fortune if you have to, but get them."

"If I can't I'll go down myself," Selkas promised. "Do you honestly think this will work, Earl?"

"It will work. Now tell Izane to set down on the back of that thing."

He had come prepared, the subjective half of the affinity-twin loaded into a large hypodermic with the longest needle obtainable. Dumarest jumped as the raft lowered, feet slipping on the moist skin of the decapod. It was like standing on the slick hull of a spaceship. He ran towards the head and the buried brain. While he had worked in the laboratory Selkas had obtained a chart of the creature's anatomy; Dumarest knew just where to dig in order to find an artery.

When he returned to the raft he was covered with blood and slime.

"Tell them to clear the area," he ordered. "Every boat and man away, fast!" He wiped himself clean with a mass of tissue. "If you lose track of this thing, Izane, I'll have your life."

The technician was offended. "There is no need of threats. I know my responsibilities."

"Just don't get careless." Dumarest moved to the rear of the raft and stripped off his tunic. "All right, Selkas."

Selkas picked up the second hypodermic. "Now?"

Dumarest looked down at the water, the sun bright on the waves, the scurrying boats looking like toys worked by miniature people. He breathed deeply, fighting his inward tension, the fear of the unknown.

"Now!"

He felt the sting of the needle.

It was a dream, a confused jumble of disassociated impressions, an incomprehensible mass of unrelated data. He was flying, no he was floating, no he was swimming, no he was drifting in clouds of limpid smoke. He was moving yet stationary, unable to distinguish fact from impression. He was afraid.

Light hurt his eyes and he tried to close them, lifting his hands to shield them when the brightness persisted. He had no hands. Instead a great veil of shadow seemed to bring relief and he felt a dull concussion. He tried again and this time the hurtful brightness vanished to be replaced by a comforting gloom. He moved again and felt a peculiar relief. Again and he saw long, prehensile arms stretching before him. Arms? His arms?

Again he knew fear.

Deliberately he fought it.

I am in this creature's brain, riding it as a man would ride a horse, yet I am not really here at all. Nothing can harm me. I am safe in the raft with Selkas. Nothing can hurt me. I am safe in the raft with Selkas. I am not really here at all.

It didn't help. Because he *was* here. He could see the thing he had become, the reality of a dreadful nightmare in which his body had become grotesquely distorted and trapped in a totally unfamiliar environment. And he wasn't alone. He could sense another entity close by as a man would sense the presence of an animal in a room: a dull bewilderment as primitive survival instincts failed to function as they should, an increasing terror as Dumarest tried to consciously control his new body.

It was the wrong method. He was a man, used to two arms, two legs, the pull of gravity. He lacked the necessary coordination to manipulate a machine with multiple limbs and a different set of responses. Given time he could have learned a certain control but there was no time and there was no need. He could dominate but he didn't have to replace. The essential habit patterns were already built into the creature's brain; he could use them merely by thinking the appropriate instructions.

He thought, *"Go down!"*

The gloom increased yet he could still see clearly, the decapod's eyes adjusting to the diminished light. A school of fish appeared before him and he swept them towards his mouth with automatic reflex, tasting nothing, not even aware of the rush of water which carried the food. And it was a normal response: how often does a man consciously direct the act of breathing?

He headed towards the shore. He didn't know in which

direction it lay but the decapod did. The water lightened and Dumarest felt a growing uneasiness. The warning mechanisms of survival reacted as they should. This region of the sea was dangerous to the creature he had become.

He overrode the cautionary signals, turning at the edge of the shelf where a wall of rock reared high before him. Eels darted from undersea caverns, jaws wide, snapping at his limbs and falling back as he lashed at the sinuous shapes. He dove deeper, trying to leave the pests behind. The gloom deepened and objects lost their sharp definition. He moved onwards looking for the cables which would mark the position of the vessel. He found one and dived for the bottom.

It looked smaller than he remembered, almost a toy as it lay in the thick ooze, and then he remembered that it wasn't small at all—it was just that the decapod had a different value of size. He approached it, sending the tentacles questing over the surface, trying to get a firm grip. Twice he failed and then the tip of one of the arms found the open port of the cargo hold. This time, when he lifted upwards, the ship came with him. He rose faster, hugging the wall, ignoring the eels which came darting to tear at his flesh. Blood streamed from a dozen places but he felt no pain. More eels appeared attracted by the scent and he rose as if surrounded by a swarm of flies. The water lightened and the edge of the shelf came into sight. He moved towards it, up and over, ship and arms scraping the bottom, higher still until the great bulk of his body scraped the bottom and the dazzling light of the sun burned his eyes.

It was impossible to get the vessel on dry land. Its weight was too great once it had lost the support of the water and he had no room in which to maneuver. He left it and pushed himself back towards the depths. Now he felt the sting of his wounds, a nagging ache from where flesh had been ripped away. He moved faster, drawing the predators away from the vessel, trailing a stream of blood and a horde of voracious eels. Undominated the decapod would have lashed at them, defending itself, finding safety in flight it it were possible or battle if it were not.

But Dumarest had no reason to keep it alive.

Trapped in the mind of the creature, it had to die before he could escape. And he had to experience every moment of its passing. He watched as the eels tore at his arms, severed portions floating past his eyes, felt the jaws rip deeper and deeper into his body, the pain mounting until it became a red tide—waiting, suffering, longing for the final dissolution.

Selkas said, "I was worried, Earl. I didn't know what to do. At first I thought you'd died and then, well, I had to use restraints."

Dumarest looked at the bruises on his arms, the welts on his body.

"You were all right at first and then you really began to struggle." Selkas wrung a cloth out in water and handed it to Dumarest. Slowly he laved his face and neck.

"Veruchia?"

"We got her out as you planned. I managed to get a couple of divers, the Ven brothers; I think they'd do anything for money. They were only just in time. The air had run out and she was unconscious, dying. They fed her air from their own tanks and got her up immediately. Izane is with her. He knows something about medicine."

162

"Did she find what she was looking for?"

"I don't know. I told you, she was unconscious and Izane gave her something to make her sleep. An anti-shock capsule. He said that she had probably accepted the concept of death and the trauma had to be overcome. But she'll be all right, thank God."

Dumarest looked at Selkas and then beyond him to where the stars shone bright against the canopy of the raft. It had been afternoon when he had entered the body of the decapod, night when he returned to his own. He leaned back, eyes misted with thought. The beast had been a long time dying. The great bulk had taken tremendous punishment and, towards the last, the primitive mind had fought with a savage intensity to stay alive. Some of that energy must have been transmitted to the subjective half of the affinity-twin. It would account for the necessity of restraints.

"I should have had you drugged, Earl, but I was afraid it might do more harm than good. I didn't know how the compound might affect the thing you had injected into your brain. I was afraid to take the chance. At times I wished that I had because you looked scarcely human. And then when Veruchia was carried to the surface and I knew that she was alive and well and would walk and talk and smile again . . . Earl! How can I thank you? What can I do?"

Dumarest rose to his feet. "The job isn't finished yet."

"What do you mean?"

"We didn't go through all this for nothing. We have until noon tomorrow for Veruchia to prove to the Council her right to inherit. Let us find out if she has that proof."

She looked very small lying on a heap of nets in a hut

close to where the waves sent ripples over the sand. The ebon tracery on her face blended with the mesh of the nets so that it seemed they covered her with their delicate strands. The bars of silver in her hair caught the light and reflected it in gleams of brightness.

Selkas looked at her, his arms aching to hold her as they had ached when she had been just a child. He resisted the temptation now as he had then. If Lisa had lived! But she had died and her memory was not to be sullied. In that bad time he had found refuge in flight, visiting a dozen worlds and thickening the armor of his assumed cynicism. Now he had to be stronger.

"I have given her a neutralizing drug," said Izane. "She will awake soon but I must repeat my warning that this is most unwise. There is a danger of disorientation and later relapse."

"Leave us." Selkas was sharp; the fool didn't know the strength of his patient. As he left Selkas dropped to his knees, one hand stroking the shining mane of hair. "Veruchia, my dear. Veruchia. Wake up, my child. My child." His words betrayed him.

"Selkas?" She smiled, sleepily. "Is it you?"

"Wake up, Veruchia."

"I had a most unusual dream," she murmured. "I thought that I had found something wonderful and then, suddenly, everything went wrong and I was alone again." Her eyes widened as memory returned. "Earl?"

"He is alive and well and looking at you this very moment."

"Earl!" She surged upright, arms extended. "Earl, my darling. You saved me. I knew that you would save me."

He felt the pressure of her lips, the heat of her body as it strained against his own. She was full of demand, a woman resurrected and filled with the desire of life. How often had he experienced the same euphoria when riding Low: the heady intoxication when the journey was safely over and he had risen from the cabinet as from a coffin.

Gently he freed the grip of her arms. "Did you find what you were looking for?"

"Earl?"

He remembered that she must still be a little confused. Patiently he said, "Was that the First Ship? Did it contain the proof you need in order to inherit?"

"Yes, Earl. Yes!" She looked wildly around. "I had a book. It was tucked under the straps of my breathing equipment. Where—"

"It will be with your equipment," said Selkas. "The Ven brothers left it in the next hut."

"Get it. Don't let it out of your sight. It is the logbook of the First Ship. Selkas, Earl, I was right! The old legends did not lie. The owner's name was Chron, not Dickarn. Dickarn was the captain but he didn't own the ship. And he wasn't the First Owner of this world. Chron died just after landing and Dickarn took over full command. He married Chron's widow and that's how the confusion began. But Chron was the First Owner. It's all in the book. I had time to read it while I was waiting."

"Before you took the quick-time?" Selkas frowned.

"After. While I waited for the ship to lift and rescue to arrive." She sighed, happily. "We won, Earl. We took a gamble and we've won. I am the new Owner of Dradea."

VIII

Montarg heard the news at dawn and within an hour was at Surat's door. Early as it was the cyber was at his desk. He rose as the visitor rushed towards him, gesturing at the acolyte who moved to step between them. Montarg was furious but there would be no need for defense. Even in his rage the man knew better than to offer violence to a servant of the Cyclan.

"You've heard?" Montarg glared at the cyber. "That bitch has found what she was looking for. Even now she is on her way to the Council and everyone expects that at noon she will be the new Owner." Rage made it impossible for him to remain still. His feet thudded on the floor as he paced the chamber. "So much for your predictions, Surat. The meanest fool in the city could have done as well."

"I do not foretell the future, my lord. I merely predict the most probable outcome of any series of events but never have I claimed to be infallible. Always there is the unknown factor."

"Excuses, cyber?"

"Facts, my lord."

"I trusted you to advise me. You predicted that I would be recognized by the Council, and what happened? Your prediction was wrong and Veruchia gained a hundred days. Again you predicted that she would not discover the First Ship, yet she did. And when she fell to the bottom trapped in the hull it seemed certain that she would die. Yet she lives. Three predictions, cyber, the last of the order of ninety-nine percent probability."

Surat's even modulation was in sharp contrast to Montarg's raving. "The decision of the Council was your own fault, my lord. Your conduct antagonized them and made them agreeable to grant the woman time to prove her claim. The discovery of the vessel was pure chance. As you will remember my prediction was ninety-two percent that she would not."

"And the last? Ninety-nine percent that she would not survive?"

"Ninety-nine percent is not certainty, my lord. Nothing can ever be certain. There is always—"

"The unknown factor," snapped Montarg, interrrupting. "In this case a man called Dumarest. He saved her. I think I shall kill him for that."

"That would be most unwise."

"Why? What is that man to you? Scum from the arena, a traveler, I should have arranged his death long ago." Montarg dropped his hand to his belt. He wore a dagger in an ornate sheath. Drawing the blade he looked at the bright steel. "I ordered a thousand of these," he said. "To be given to graduates as a symbol of the new culture of this world." Abruptly he threw the weapon, the blade quivering as it buried its point in the desk. "Veruchia," he said. "That bitch will never be the Owner."

Surat looked at his desk. The knife was inches from

where his hand rested on the surface but he had no effort to move it, predicting the path of the blade even as Montarg had thrown it. A stupid, emotional gesture without logic or reason, typical of the man and typical of all those who were slaves to glandular secretions. How could such people hope to control the destiny of worlds? How could they formulate policies and determine actions when, at any moment, they could fall victim to hate and fear and anger? Emotion was insanity.

And yet it could be used. Surat pondered. Would it be best to allow the man to kill Veruchia? The Council would take revenge, true, but his son would inherit and regents be found to hold the planet in trust—the Council, perhaps, there were precedents. But such an arrangement would complicate matters. One man was easier to guide than many and the central intelligence had ordered a speeding-up of the program. So Montarg must inherit.

He watched as the man retrieved his dagger and thrust it back into its sheath. The act of throwing it seemed to have acted as a catharsis and when he spoke it was in a tone calmer than before.

"Make me a prediction, cyber. What is the probability that Veruchia will inherit?"

"If she has the necessary proof, my lord, and my informants tell me she has, the probability of her becoming the new Owner is almost certain."

"Wrong." Montarg gave his silent laugh. "Her ancestry is in doubt. I have reason to believe that Oued was not her father. A biological examination of her genetic factors could prove it beyond question. Amplon could do it. The old fool would have no choice if the Council made a direct order. I'll get on to him now. Where is your phone."

He reached the instrument before Surat could object, punched a number, spoke, waited with a frown. Again he snapped into the instrument, his voice rising with mounting impatience. When finally he turned away his eyes were puzzled.

"Amplon is dead."

Amplon and Redal both, the one as a precaution, the other because he had failed. Placed in the laboratory for one reason only, he had missed the chance when it came. He had failed to obtain the correct sequence of molecular units and the Cyclan had no time for those who did not succeed. His body was in the pool weighed with lead.

"It is no loss, my lord," said Surat evenly. "He would not have been able to help you."

"There are others. We can send for a biotechnician if necessary. I'm convinced that Selkas fathered Lisa's child."

"Even so it makes no difference, my lord. Her claim is based on the maternal, not the paternal side. Lisa was in direct descent from Chron and there is no doubt that Veruchia is her child."

"Then she must die. And the man Dumarest with her."

"No, my lord. Not the man."

Surat could not feel emotion and his voice was always evenly modulated but, even so, Montarg sensed a peculiar strain. Curiously he studied the thin face, the hard, almost stonelike features beneath the shaven skull, his innate intuition jumping gaps of logic and arriving at an instinctive conclusion.

Surat kept insisting that Dumarest remain unharmed.

Why? What possible reason could the cyber have for
protecting such a man? What connection could there be
between a common traveler, a fighter in the arena and
the world-embracing organization of the Cyclan?

Quietly he said, "Dumarest. The unknown factor.
There is a mystery as to how Veruchia was rescued. Dumarest, somehow, seemed to have managed to control the
actions of a decapod. Yes, I have my informants, too. I
was kept notified." He frowned, thinking. "Both Dumarest and Selkas visited the biological laboratory. A
series of experiments was discontinued and the entire resources of the building concentrated on the manufacture
of fifteen molecular units. A member of the staff thought
I should know, he was eager to maintain good relations
with the next Owner." He scowled. "The next probable
Owner. I thought him a fool, but now I am not so sure.
And now Amplon is dead and his assistant nowhere to be
found. A mystery, Surat, don't you agree?"

"A series of unrelated incidents, my lord."

"Such talk from a cyber? Can any series of incidents
be unrelated?" Montarg stood, brooding, unaware of the
acolyte edging close, ready to send a poisoned dart into
his flesh if Surat should give the signal, a poison which
would kill, not immediately, but in a hour when he was
safely away and no suspicion would be aroused.

"Dumarest has something you want," he said abruptly.
"A secret of some kind. I can think of no other explanation why you insist he must remain unharmed. Fifteen
units—assembled in a certain order, perhaps? Is that it?"

His intuition was incredible; somehow he had stumbled on the correct answer. A guess, perhaps, but one
which would normally have earned him immediate
death. A gesture and the thing would be done, but Surat

did not give the signal. Montarg was more fortunate than he could ever suspect.

The Cyclan had made plans for this world and he was a part of them. The need for haste dictated that he inherit and Surat was a devoted servant of the organization which he served. Yet if he became certain that Dumarest was of prime importance to the Cyclan he would have a weapon against them. It was a dilemma which had to be resolved.

"Fifteen units," Montarg said again. "But no, if it were simply a matter of finding the correct order you could try them all."

Any mathematician would reveal his error.

"The possible number of combinations of fifteen units runs into millions, my lord. If it were possible to try one new sequence each second it would take four thousand years to test them all."

"Then he does have the secret?"

It was time for a little truth. "Yes, my lord. A thing stolen from the Cyclan."

"And you want it back." Montarg threw back his head as he gave his silent laugh. "A bargain, cyber. See that I inherit and I will tell you how to get what you want."

His intuition had failed him. He did not realize that he was offering to give away the greatest power a man could know.

The house was as she remembered. The flowers wilted, dead in the vases, but otherwise everything was the same. Veruchia stood for a moment in the hall, relaxing in the familiar embrace, little things sharply clear: a toy she had cherished as a child; a picture framed and hanging a little askew on a wall; a dish made of shells collected on a bright day when, as a child, she had first seen the awesome expanse of the sea.

Selkas caught her arm as she made to run from the hall into the rooms.

"A moment."

"But this is my house! Surely I am safe here?"

"You haven't inherited yet," said Dumarest. "There are still two hours to noon. Wait here until I check."

She frowned as he moved from room to room. Was it always going to be like this? Fearing every shadow in case it had a lurking assassin? Did every ruler have to be surrounded by guards and watchful eyes? She relaxed as Dumarest returned, throwing off the momentary chill. This was her home and in it she was safe, as she would always be safe while he was at her side.

Selkas watched as she left the hall, seeing her smile, her undisguised pleasure.

"She is happy," he said. "I have never seen her so radiant. Not even when I called to take you both to the Council. She was happy then, but this is something I have wished for all her life."

Dumarest said, "Your daughter?"

"You guessed." Selkas drew in his breath. "She must never know. Lisa was a wonderful woman and Oued was my friend. There was a time of sweet madness—I make no excuses. Do you love her?"

"In a matter of hours she will own a world."

"And you are a man and you have your pride. But I think that you love her, Earl. Why else did you risk your life?"

"For information."

"Only that?" Selkas smiled his disbelief. "Well, no matter. Shall we wait in the study?"

The book Veruchia had found lay on the desk, old, stained with water, the writing cramped and precise. Dumarest leafed through it as Selkas poured two glasses of brandy. He shook his head at the offered drink.

"No thank you."

"Disappointed, Earl?"

The book contained nothing but the record of the journey, the account of the first few years. The navigational tables he had hoped to find were gone, carried away by the gush of air when the port had been opened, perhaps, or taken out of the ship years ago. Yet there were clues.

"This world was settled from a planet named Hensh," said Selkas. "There is mention of Quell and Allmah, but nothing of Earth."

Three planets. Dumarest hunted through the book looking for their reference. The captain had been stringently precise. Each world carried a set of figures after the name.

"Selkas, is there a planetary almanac here?"

"I don't know. Shall I ask Veruchia?"

"Never mind." Dumarest was at the shelves, searching. He pulled a thick volume from where it rested and carried it back to the desk. Quickly he leafed through it. "Hensh," he said. "Selkas! The coordinates are not the same!"

"Are you certain?"

"Look for yourself." Dumarest's finger stabbed at the almanac and then at the notation in the log book. He riffled more pages. "Quell and Allmah, both the same. Neither has a modern reference." He leaned back, thinking. "The ship must have used the original navigational tables. That is why the coordinates given are not the same as those now used."

"In that case—" Selkas broke off what he was about to suggest. "No, Earl. It must be a mistake. A private code of the captain, perhaps. They needn't be coordinates at all."

Dumarest wasn't listening. He looked at the stained pages and the three sets of figures the long-dead captain had left. Had that man known Earth? Had he been able to look at the sky and single out the star which warmed the planet he yearned to find?

Three sets of figures; three items of information which could be fed into a computer for the machine to devise an analogue of the tables from which they must have come, tables which would have used as their zero-point the region he needed to find—the planet Earth, perhaps, it was possible.

Home!

Dumarest looked at his hands. They trembled a little and he reached for the brandy Selkas had poured, warming the goblet between his palms. A journey to a planet selling computer services; a wait while the analogue was constructed and comparisons made and then, at last, his search could be over.

Success made him dizzy.

No, not success.

He looked at the untouched brandy in his hands, at the figure of Selkas slumped in a chair, and surged to his feet.

"Veruchia!"

"What is it, darling?" She was casual, unaware of danger. "Earl?"

She reached the study as men burst into the hall.

"A neat little house," said Montarg. "Small and snug and nicely warm. A fit setting for a pearl even if it is flawed." He moved restlessly about the hall, alive with bursting energy. "A neat trick as I think you'll agree. A hole bored through the wall and a gas fed into the atmosphere. Simple, quick and efficient. The men were hardly necessary but Surat insisted that I use caution. Right, cyber?"

"The unexpected must always be anticipated, my lord."

"So we brought men with us just in case your tame dog could do without breathing, Veruchia." Montarg paused behind her chair. "Are you comfortable, cousin?" He tightened the strap a little. "Better now?"

She refused to give him satisfaction, sitting with tight lips as the strap binding her body and arms to the back of the chair dug into her flesh. He scowled, taking up another notch.

"Well, scum of the arena? Aren't you going to plead for your slut?"

Dumarest ignored him, looking about the hall. Like Veruchia he was strapped to a chair, the broad leather band holding his upper arms close to his body, his body tight to the wooden back. Selkas was nowhere to be seen. Aside from Veruchia and Montarg the hall was deserted but for the cyber and one of his acolytes. The men who had rushed into the house had been sent away. The gas which had robbed him of strength dissipated.

"Answer me when I speak!" Montarg stepped forward, the back of his hand lashing across Dumarest's face. A ring he wore caught the lip and sent blood into his mouth.

Dumarest said, "Is this what you call the mystique of combat?"

"You mock me?"

"To torture a helpless woman and to beat a helpless man." Dumarest spat a mouthful of blood. It landed on Montarg's foot. "You are a brave warrior, my lord."

Rage drew Montarg's face into a livid mask. He raised his hand again and sent the ring to tear a furrow across Dumarest's check. As it landed he kicked at the floor and sent the chair slipping across the polished wood to slam against the wall. Montarg followed and the acolyte moved forward a little as he raised his hand to strike a third blow.

"My lord." Surat's even modulation was like water thrown on a fire. "We waste time. The Council is due to assemble in an hour. It would be most unwise to keep it waiting."

"They will wait. They have no choice."

"Even so, my lord, we have no time to waste."

Montarg sneered. "What you really mean is that you don't want me to hurt your property. All right, cyber, I understand." He looked down at Dumarest. "Listen, you filth. You have a secret the cyber wants to learn. You will tell him what he wants to know or the girl will suffer."

Dumarest glanced to where Surat stood like a living flame in the scarlet of his robe. He and Montarg working in partnership? It was impossible, the Cyclan admitted of no equal. Montarg was being used, then, manipulated to the cyber's ends. He tensed the muscles of arms and shoulders. The chair felt like a rock.

Flatly he said, "Why should that worry me?"

"Because she is soft and helpless and you are a fool.

Because you are in love with her and would hate to see her flayed alive."

Dumarest shrugged. "She is only a woman. My secret is worth a million of them."

It was logic the cyber could appreciate. Montarg's promise had depended on the power of emotion and Surat had no means of calculating the power of love. He had never known it and could never know it. And now there was no need of Montarg's further help. He had Dumarest and what was in his mind could be learned.

"My lord, this has gone far enough. With your permission I will take the man and go."

"If you do you won't get far, cyber." Montarg was grim. Also he was curious; if the secret were so important he wanted to know it. "I've men outside and they have their orders. If you leave without me they will hold you. They might even kill you and the man you value so much also. We'll do this my way, as we agreed."

"Your way is not working, my lord."

"It'll work. Don't be deluded by what he said. I know better and so does the woman. Once she begins to scream, he'll soon talk."

"Earl?" Veruchia was puzzled. "What's this all about? What is it he wants to know?"

"Shut your mouth," snapped Montarg.

Dumarest rammed him in the stomach.

He threw himself forward, using the weight of the chair to accentuate his own, his head landing just above the groin. Before Montarg had fallen he had jerked backwards, slamming the chair against the wall. The construction was solid. It did not break though he felt the joints yield a little. Before he could try again the acolyte had run forward, holding him firm with irresistible strength.

Montarg was strangely calm. He rose, breathing heavily, a thin patina of sweat shining on his face. He walked towards Veruchia flexing his hands. He gripped.

She screamed.

The screams rose to shrieks interspersed with a frantic pleading. "Don't! Please don't. Earl, help me!"

He strained, feeling the strap yield a little, the back of the chair begin to break.

The shrieks became a raw sound of agony. Dumarest felt the sweat on his face, the sting as it touched the gash on his cheek and the cut on his lip. The acolyte stared at him with detached interest and he forced himself to be patient. Too soon and they would be suspicious. Too late and he would have caused the girl unnecessary pain.

Montarg stepped away from the chair and looked at Veruchia. She slumped, whimpering, the sound of an animal hurt and not knowing why.

"I think you must be enjoying this, Dumarest." His face held a satiated expression. "But unless you talk soon she will never be normal again. I am giving her a respite, otherwise she will faint and so escape my attentions. In a short while I will begin removing the skin from her face and body. The design she carries will make it interesting. Alternate patches, yes? An art form of red and white edged with black. But now there is a little something I have often wanted to try."

Her shriek tore the air.

"No!" Dumarest surged against his bonds. "Leave her alone. I'll tell you what you want to know."

"You see, cyber?" Montarg was triumphant. "The

power of love. It is strong enough to overcome even his reluctance to yield the secret."

"That we shall see, my lord."

"You doubt it?" Montarg smiled. "He knows better than to lie. If he hopes to gain time or a respite for his woman he will regret it. The next time I shall not stop so soon. Well, Dumarest? What is this precious knowledge."

"The sequence of the molecular units forming the affinity-twin," said Dumarest quickly. Had he known? From his expression Dumarest guessed he had. But the rest? "It enabled me to control the decapod."

"Some form of hypnotic chemical?" Montarg shrugged. "Well, tell the cyber and get it over with."

He didn't know. For a moment Dumarest was tempted to try and set one against the other, to bribe Montarg with golden promises, but he knew that it would be of no use. He would be suspicious of such an obvious attempt to win his support.

Instead he said, "And afterwards? What happens then?"

"Nothing. Both you and the woman will be set free."

He was lying. Veruchia would be killed and himself taken by the Cyclan. Surat would never trust him to give the correct sequence. He would be held while tests were made, his brain probed for the true information. The cyber must have his own reasons for this farce.

"I'll have to write it down," said Dumarest. "You'll have to free my arms."

"That will be unnecessary. You have movement enough." Surat nodded at his acolyte. "Give him paper and something with which to write."

It was a stylo, long, slender, the point tapering to an

ink-loaded ball. Dumarest scrawled the symbols in random order, accentuating his difficulty.

"Show me." Montarg moved close as Surat studied the paper. "Is that the secret? I want a copy."

"Certainly, my lord." Surat had anticipated the demand. "He will write you one."

Dumarest crouched over the paper. Surat was being subtle. It was hard to remember fifteen units scrawled at random. If the second copy did not match the first it would prove it false. If it did he would have a point to work on should anything happen to rob him of his source of information.

"Let me see!" Montarg snatched the paper. "Are they the same?" Both men concentrated on the scrawled symbols.

It was the moment Dumarest had waited for. He surged, the soles of his feet hard against the floor, the muscles of loins and back cracking as he fought to straighten against the cramping bulk of the chair. Wood shattered, weakened by the previous blows, the chair disintegrating into its various parts.

As the acolyte grabbed at him Dumarest's hand rose, the stylo resting against his palm, the point shearing into the eye and the brain beneath.

"No!" Surat jumped before Montarg as he clawed at the laser in his sleeve. If Dumarest should be killed his life was ended, his future, the reward of being assimilated into central intelligence.

"Stand aside, you fool!" Montarg had the gun out, the barrel leveling as Dumarest tore free the hampering strap. "Stand aside!"

He swore as the cyber still blocked his aim and ran to where Veruchia sagged against her bonds. Dumarest lunged towards him. He saw the gun steady its aim, the whiteness of Montarg's knuckle as he pressed the trigger.

The first shot missed. The second burned a groove on the slope of his shoulder and then he was on the man, his left hand flashing out to grip the weapon, to raise and turn it as Montarg fired again. He heard the hiss of seared flesh and twisted, seeing Surat fall, a charred hole in the shaven expanse of his skull.

Dumarest dropped his free hand to the dagger in its ornate sheath, lifted it, held it so the light shone on the blade.

"No! Please, no!"

"For Veruchia, Montarg," said Dumarest.

And slammed the dagger into his heart.

The city was celebrating. Lights shone on every building and the streets were full of people, men and women dancing to the tune of wandering musicians, wine and food free at every intersection. Riding high above the noise and confusion Veruchia could hardly believe that it was all for her.

"An old tradition," said Selkas. "Each new Owner is expected to squander some rent in providing a feast. When Chorzel inherited he offered land to every man who could run to the Ulam Depression and back in a day. Three managed to do it." He fell silent, thinking. "That was before he instigated the games."

"What made him do it, Selkas?"

"Send men to die in the arena? You've heard all the reasons many times."

Dumarest said, "He was guided by the Cyclan. You need no better reason than that."

He sat beside the canopy, not looking at the others,

not wanting to be with them, but Veruchia had insisted. She had been Owner for a day and had still to learn that rule carried responsibility. And she had still to realize the danger which lurked and would always lurk, waiting to trap the unwary.

"Surat gave him bad advice," said Selkas. "Is that what you mean?"

"I mean that the Cyclan deliberately tried to ruin this world and they've almost done it. Had Montarg inherited they would have succeeded. You don't need me to tell you that. You have a civilized culture here and it has been contaminated by barbaric influences. You've traveled, Selkas, you know. It takes little to veer the course of a planet's progress. Without commerce, ships don't call and without ships there is an inevitable indrawing and stagnation. It's your job, Veruchia, to alter the trend. Shut the area or, better, let it be for honest sport. Real games, not festivals of blood."

Dumarest thought of Sadoua. His life was the arena. Well, life was a constant struggle. He would survive.

"But why?" asked Veruchia. "What possible reason could the Cyclan have for wanting this world to become so isolated?"

Dumarest looked at the stars; they were dimmed by the brilliance from below. But the question had started a train of thought. The Cyclan did nothing without reason. Their iron logic dictated that everything they did moved to a determined end and he knew how devious they could be.

He said, slowly, "This is a theory, nothing more. What happens when a world progresses? Commerce increases, the population grows, ships are plentiful and, if there are suitable worlds nearby, they too will share in the expansion. It could be that the Cyclan didn't want Dradea to become viable to prevent that very thing."

Which meant the organization did not want this sector of space to become too well-traversed. Did they have something to hide? A sector they wished to keep isolated? A world which had to remain untouched?

Earth, perhaps?

He sat brooding as the raft sloped across the sky to settle at the edge of the city before familiar walls.

"Home," said Veruchia. "My home."

Not the palace: that was too large, too overwhelming as yet, and for reasons of her own she wanted the privacy of familiar surroundings. Selkas knew what was in her mind and was smoothly diplomatic.

"I'll call for you tomorrow," he said. "There's a lot to be done and you'll have to move into the palace in order to do it. Then there is the Council to meet and decisions to be made. I'll see you too, Earl. There are certain matters to be settled."

Money, his pay and, perhaps, other things.

"We can do it now," said Dumarest. "I'll come with you."

"Tomorrow will do. Tonight Veruchia needs you."

Dumarest looked at the girl where she stood before the open door of her house. She turned, smiling before passing inside. Around the walls inconspicuous men stood quietly on watch. There was no longer any need for him to guard against assassins. The Owner of a world did not lack bodyguards.

"She loves you," said Selkas evenly. "Surely you know that. And she needs strength and reassurance if she is to rule this world and guide it the way it must go. You can give her that strength, Earl. You must."

"Must?"

"Have you never been in love, Earl? Don't you know what it is to have one person fill your world? To think of your future always with that one person in mind?" Selkas caught Dumarest's expression and was suddenly contrite. "I'm sorry. I've wakened hurtful memories. You must forgive me."

Dumarest looked at the house, the canopy, the hard lines of his reflection. The dead should not be able to hurt so much—not when they had loved so deep.

"When Lisa died I thought I would go mad," whispered Selkas. "I couldn't believe that I would never see her again. Always she was around the next corner, in the next room, but she never was. And always, always, she haunts my dreams. I don't want that to happen to Veruchia. Not now, not yet, not ever if it can be avoided. In her life she has known too much sorrow. Don't add to it, Earl. Go to her. She needs you."

She was singing as he entered the house, a lilting melody reflecting her happiness. She called out as he closed the door and stood leaning against it, looking at the hall. The blood had gone, the broken chair, the bodies he had left lying. Only a seared patch on a wall and another on the polished floor told of the violence this place had known.

"Earl? Is that you, my darling?"

"Yes, Veruchia."

"So formal! Has Selkas gone?"

"Yes."

He moved into the study and helped himself to brandy, warming the goblet as he looked at the ranked books and the ancient maps. One, more modern, was that of Dradea, and he stood looking at it as he sipped the brandy. The desert of Wend, the glacier of Cosne, the broad expanse of the Elgish Sea where they both had nearly died—where he had died.

He drank, more deeply this time, not wanting to remember the pain, the growing darkness, the last wash of oblivion. Was death really like that? Would it come again as it had before? Or would it come quick and fast, unsuspected and merciful in lack of anticipation?

The goblet was empty. He refilled it and again studied the map. Dradea was a fair world with great potential. A city could be built there. Another at the foot of those hills. A port could fit into that natural harbor and spacefields could stretch in a dozen places.

"It's a beautiful planet, Earl. And it's all ours."

"Yours, Veruchia."

"Ours, darling. Yours and mine."

She had changed and was wearing a thin robe of gossamer, laced down the front, open at the shoulders, the black lace merging with the natural adornment of her flesh so that it was hard to see where the one ended and the other began. Her hair streamed loose and silken, silver against jet, comet trails against a midnight sky. Her eyes were luminous. Her lips were full and faintly moist. It seemed incredible that he had ever likened her to a boy.

"Yours and mine," she repeated. "We share it. There was a bargain, remember?"

One made after a night of love when she had been desperate for his help. But at least she had remembered. She was a woman who would never forget anything.

"No," he said. "Shared responsibility never works and what would I do with half a planet? You keep it. You won it and it's yours."

188

She didn't argue, knowing as he did the dissension which would arise, the cabals formed by those jealous of a stranger. And Montarg's son would provide a nucleus for rebellion.

"Then I'll make you a High Tenant with land enough to make you independent and money enough so that you can do as you please."

It was good to have power, to make decisions and to give rewards. She watched as Dumarest poured brandy into a glass, taking it as he lifted his own.

"A toast, Veruchia. To the most beautiful Owner this world has ever known. The most beautiful it could ever have."

She felt herself grow hot with pleasure and was suddenly conscious of the thing which had set her apart. He caught the hand which lifted, unconsciously, to her face.

"No, Veruchia, I want to see you while I have the chance. Within a week every woman on this planet will have copied your markings. The price of fame, my dear. They will all want to look like the Owner. But only the Owner will be unique."

"Earl! My darling!"

The goblet fell as she moved into his arms, the brandy spilling unheeded on the floor. She wound her arms around his neck and pressed against him with mounting demand. He responded and happiness suffused her like a flood.

He would stay.

For a while, at least, he would stay.

He would forget his dream of finding Earth, of returning home. Home was where the heart resided and soon he would accept that.

"Earl?"

"Darling?"

"You'll never leave me?"

She felt the sudden tension, the reluctance to answer and closed his lips with her own before he could reply. He had traveled all his life and it was a habit hard to break. The time would come when he would yearn to be on his way again, looking, searching, moving from world to world. He might even go, it was a chance she had to take. A bigger chance that, if he did, he would return.

But he wouldn't go tonight.

He wouldn't go tomorrow.

He might never go at all. He wouldn't be the first man who had lost a world for the love of a woman.

MORE SCIENCE FICTION! *ADVENTURE*

BEST-SELLING
Science Fiction
and
Fantasy